The Enchanted Riddle

The Enchanted Riddle

Charlotte Kandel

www.stridentpublishing.co.uk

Published by
Strident Publishing Ltd
22 Strathwhillan Drive
The Orchard, Hairmyres
East Kilbride G75 8GT

Tel: +44 (0)1355 220588
info@stridentpublishing.co.uk
www.stridentpublishing.co.uk

Published by Strident Publishing Limited, 2012
Text © Charlotte Kandel, 2012
Cover design by Susan Pierce Sloan

A catalogue record for this book is
available from the British Library.

ISBN 978-1-905537-33-7

Typeset in Dante MT Std by
Palimpsest Book Production Limited, Falkirk, Stirlingshire
Printed by CPI Group (UK) Ltd

ALBA | CHRUTHACHAIL

The publisher acknowledges support from Creative
Scotland towards the publication of this title

Acknowledgements

FOR STANLEY AND DIANA AND DESMOND

Without the three people named above there would
be no Daphne at all. I love you all.
I also send love and deepest gratitude to my talented,
determined agent, Linda Langton.
And at Strident, Keith, Alison and Anna have provided
more help, enthusiasm and good fun than any writer
could imagine. Thank you so very much.

PART ONE

First, you must find me.

Chapter One

The luncheon bell clanged gloomily through the dim corridors of the Orphanage of Saint Jude. From all over the old building the girls, aged from five to sixteen, began to collect outside the dining hall. In their drab grey uniforms they all looked the same, dreary and colourless. Just like St. Jude's itself.

St. Jude's wasn't a harsh place. It was really quite kind. It was just that sadness and boredom hung in the air like a sour smell. The 'babies' were allowed to laugh and play games, but when the 'grown up' age of five was reached life became a serious matter. Fun, so desperately longed for, hardly ever happened.

Below the dining hall, in the dusty basement gym, a slender figure leaped energetically through the air. Daphne's long, shining dark brown hair streamed out behind her as she danced. Her face, with its creamy olive skin and enormous dark eyes, wore a look of total, concentrating bliss. Deaf to the bell's summons, she flew in graceful movement down the narrow room. Humming, she was completely lost in her imagination. Her diamond-scattered skirt floated around her as she danced. In the gold-encrusted theatre, with its deep red velvet seats, the applause grew to a deafening roar.

"Daphne!" A quiet voice spoke from the doorway. Daphne came down to earth with a startled bump. The packed theatre and its cheering audience vanished abruptly.

"Didn't you hear the bell?" asked Sister Mary Euphoria, St. Jude's popular young music mistress. "Lunch."

"Can I just do one more quick length of the gym? And could you watch me, Sister, and tell me if you think my landings are getting steadier?" Daphne pleaded.

"Sorry, Daphne. Now. You know you're supposed to set an example to the junior girls."

Sister Mary Euphoria reached into the pocket of her black habit and pulled out some hairpins. "Put your hair up tidily. We're late." With her hands firmly placed on Daphne's reluctant shoulders, the nun gave her a friendly squeeze and steered her into the corridor.

"Oh, cruel Messenger of Fate. My ballet career means nothing to you," Daphne cried. She staggered backwards, her hand pressed to her forehead.

Mary Euphoria smiled affectionately. "And which of

4

the hundreds of books you've taken out of the school library inspired you to utter those deathless phrases?"

Daphne, caught, grinned back, and snapped briskly out of her touching swoon. "All right then, I'm coming, but at least tell me whether or not the rumours are true."

Sister Mary Euphoria never pretended she didn't know what you were talking about, nor was she stingy with information.

"Yes," she said cautiously. "They're true. There *is* a family applying to adopt an older girl. Apparently, the poor mother's had to give up on having a daughter of her own, and the family all feel it's too late for them to bring up a baby."

Daphne's eyes widened. It was well known at St. Jude's that everyone wanted babies to adopt. The older you got the less chance there was that anyone would choose *you*. Daphne's mind seethed with questions. Watching her excited face Mary Euphoria said gently, "That's all I know, I promise."

They entered the dining hall, where the subdued voices of more than two hundred girls echoed. Daphne slid in on her class's bench next to her best friend, Felicity, while Sister Mary Euphoria took up her place at the table's head. Making a face at the soggy sausages, grey mashed potatoes and pile of wilted cabbage on the plate in front of her, Daphne slowly began to eat.

Then, she saw her arch-enemy, the elderly Sister Pauline Emmanuel, trudging past the table with the day's post. *There won't be anything for me*, Daphne thought, with her usual shiver of disappointment. There never had been; not once in the thirteen years since she'd been found outside St. Jude's front door, with a note pinned to her baby shawl, which had read simply: *My name is Daphne*.

Her mind drifted away to the interesting question of why, exactly, Sister Pauline Emmanuel hated her so much. She was startled by an excited nudge from the girl next to her. "Daphne! Wake up! The Reverend Mother wants you."

Stunned, Daphne walked, a seemingly endless walk, to the front of the long room.

"How nice, Daphne. Something for you today," the Mother Superior said. She held out a brown paper parcel tied with the most beautiful silver lace string.

Daphne grasped the flat package, her mind whirling. Someone from the outside world had sent this to her. *Who?* Could today be the day she'd dreamed of, the day she'd longed for, when at last she'd find out where she really belonged? Without knowing how she got there, she was back at her seat with everyone talking to her at once. "Daphne, who's it from?" "Oh my goodness, those are Italian stamps? And the postmark says Rome — *look*." "You *lucky* thing."

Daphne's hands were trembling so much she couldn't undo the knots. "I can't make my hands work properly," she said, her voice sounding odd and squeaky. "Would you do it, Sister?"

"I'll save this pretty silver string," Sister Mary Euphoria said. At last Daphne held the package again in her own hands. The table fell completely silent as she undid the wrapping.

It was a book. The cover showed a young ballerina in a floating white dress, a sparkling diamond tiara in her dark hair. She was in graceful mid-air flight, one leg stretched out perfectly ahead of her, the other behind her. Her arms were held in a graceful arc above her head.

Daphne's eyes sparkled like candle flames. *"How to Teach Yourself Ballet,"* she read the title aloud in wonder, because this was what *she* had just been trying to do in the gym. Did some mysterious person out there in the world know about her lifelong dream of being a ballerina? Know that she'd danced before she could talk, making up her own steps?

Turning page after page, Daphne's heart sang a song of joy. She'd never seen real dancers, of course. But the book had so many photographs. Some of the dancers were even her age! There they all were in rehearsal clothes, warming-up and practising steps; and glory of glories, in the most beautiful costumes dancing on glittering stages. "Now I can learn how to dance properly," she whispered. Eagerly, she pulled the wrappings apart, looking for the letter of explanation that surely must be there.

There *was* more in the parcel, but it wasn't a letter. It was something small and soft, wrapped in fragile old tissue paper. With extreme care Daphne opened it.

Bafflingly, the tissue paper held a pair of old-fashioned scarlet silk stockings. "Who on earth has sent me *these?*"

"Perhaps they go with the book," Sister Mary Euphoria suggested.

"Well, if they do, Sister, I don't understand why. Am I supposed to put the stockings on and dance? That can't be right. None of the girls in the photographs are wearing red stockings." She handed *How to Teach Yourself Ballet* to Felicity. "Look."

Felicity intently turned the pages. "You're right," she agreed.

"Their tights are all white or pale pink. It's a mystery isn't it?"

As the beautiful book was passed around the table

Daphne sat, deep in thought, holding the stockings in her hands.

And then it happened. Was it her imagination or could she really feel heat surging out from the stockings, warming the palms of her hands like a friendly greeting?

Startled, she dropped the stockings and searched through the parcel again. But there was nothing else. Not so much as a single sheet of paper.

"Look inside the book," Mary Euphoria said, her eyes on Daphne's disappointed face. "There may be a message written in it for you."

There was. On the book's first blank page Daphne saw five lines of faint, elegant handwriting in silver ink.

"It looks like a riddle!" Her voice shook as she read it out loud:

> *First, you must find me.*
> *Then, you must follow me.*
> *Choosing, you will test me.*
> *Knowing, you will challenge me.*
> *At last, you must deserve me.*

Bewildered, Daphne raised her eyes from the page. "What can it possibly *mean?*" she asked.

Chapter Two

Immediately after lunch Daphne had to go to Sister Pauline Emmanuel's French class. "Ten minutes to wash our hands after lunch, then the bell for afternoon classes, then our walk, then tea, then mending our uniforms and knitting, then supper, then study hour, then bed," she muttered to her friend Felicity at the next desk. "We never have any time to ourselves to think." She clutched the ballet book in her hands.

If only she could disappear somewhere by herself to puzzle over the riddle. But instead, here she was, stuck in a boring class. Crossly, she opened the lid of her wooden desk and put her parcel inside while Sister Pauline Emmanuel wrote stolidly on the blackboard. "I just can't see the point of sitting here," Daphne whispered to Felicity. "I'm going to be a ballerina and ballerinas don't waste their time learning French, they dance!"

Warily, Daphne raised the lid of her desk and, hidden

behind it, opened *How to Teach Yourself Ballet*. Immediately, she lost all track of where she was.

"What's the French word for *hedgehog*?" Sister Pauline Emmanuel rasped in Daphne's ear. The nun had crept up so close Daphne could see the horrible black hairs in her bulgy nostrils.

Daphne jumped, and her desk lid slammed shut. "Je m'excuse ma soeur," she said, hoping that apologising in French would calm Sister Pauline Emmanuel down. Worse luck, it didn't.

"After the bell this afternoon, Mademoiselle Daphne," the nun said grimly, "you will take this piece of chalk and write three hundred times on the blackboard "J'aime bien les herissons."

"But Sister, please, after French it's gym and I'm allowed to dance," Daphne said urgently.

"Not today you won't be dancing. Today you will stay in this room and tell me three hundred times how very much you like hedgehogs," said Sister Pauline Emmanuel with a satisfied smirk. Ignoring Daphne's stricken face, the nun plodded back to the blackboard.

Cautiously, Daphne leaned over towards Felicity again and whispered, "Why does Sister P. loathe me, do you think?"

"Probably because she's never had a day's fun in her

life and even in this dungeon you manage to have some!" Felicity whispered back sympathetically.

The French class dragged on to its end. When the bell finally rang the girls jumped up and thundered out. Sister Pauline Emmanuel immediately called them back and ordered them to leave again, this time with decorum. Then she handed a piece of chalk to Daphne. "Three hundred lines should take you approximately two hours to write, Mademoiselle. If you hurry you might be able to get to the dining hall in time for tea." As the nun strode out, Daphne started writing as fast as she could. Tea was the one decent meal of the day. It had cake.

Her chest tightened in a combination of anger and crushing boredom. It was *so* unfair. Everyone at St. Jude's knew of her dream to learn how to dance and to be a ballerina. She *had* to practise every day.

Then she had an idea. She darted over to her desk and got her book. In a corner of the blackboard, she wrote the mysterious five-line riddle. It was better after that because, while her hand scribbled the stupid hedgehog sentence over and over, she was really puzzling over what *First, you must find me*, might mean. By the time the blackboard was covered with her miniature writing, she'd worked out an exciting explanation.

It's a treasure hunt, she told herself. *It must be.*

The bell rang for tea. Daphne quickly wiped the riddle from the blackboard, gathered up her precious parcel and ran.

She spent the rest of the day opening drawers and peering into cupboards until, with the other girls, she climbed the creaking staircase to the dormitories. She didn't know what she was looking for and she hadn't found anything at all unusual. But it didn't matter. It was the beginning of having a secret, something exciting to look forward to.

The chilly dormitory contained ten identical metal beds, each with its own white woollen blanket dropping to touch the bare wooden floor. Every girl had a small bedside chest for her few possessions. The girls were allowed ten minutes to get undressed before the lights-out bell. After that it was strictly forbidden to talk or get out of bed again, unless you had to go the bathroom along the dark, freezing corridor.

Daphne undressed with frantic speed, using a method she'd invented one icy winter. Everyone else copied it now. First you took off your lace-up shoes and school tie, next you unbuttoned the top two buttons of your shirt, and then pulled everything else, except your underwear, off over your head in one go. You got under the covers, then you took off your underwear and put on your nightgown, hoarding whatever miserly warmth you could hold onto.

At last Daphne was ready for the moment she'd longed for all day. Sitting on her bed, she unfolded one of the scarlet stockings and slid it carefully onto her foot. With a soft, murmuring sound, almost as if it were alive, it moved and shaped itself perfectly to her. She put on the matching stocking and turned her legs this way and that, admiring their blaze of colour in the dim light of her bedside lamp.

The other girls gathered round. "They look like they were made especially for you," Felicity said, awed.

The lights-out handbell clanged deafeningly, swung by Sister Pauline Emmanuel as she marched into the dorm. The girls scattered. Instinctively, Daphne leapt under the covers. *I'm not giving her a chance to tell me to take them off*, she thought, crossly.

"No more talking. Lamps out," the Sister said brusquely, banging the door shut behind her.Daphne held her breath until the last clang died away, then, in answer to the whispered requests, she got up and went from bed to bed showing off the stockings and letting everyone feel how soft and silky they were.

Suddenly, a torch blazed in the doorway. For the second time that day Sister Pauline Emmanuel had caught

Daphne breaking the rules. "DAPHNE, isn't one severe reprimand enough today? Why are you out of bed?"

"Just going to the bathroom, Sister."

"Well go then, and don't wander around keeping everyone else awake."

Daphne couldn't believe Sister Pauline Emmanuel hadn't noticed the scarlet stockings. Wearing something not on the strict uniform list should have earned her another stinging rebuke at the very least!

She glanced down at her legs. The stockings! They'd vanished! What on earth was happening? She hadn't taken them off, she hadn't had time to. Where were they? She groped for the nearest bedpost and clung to its comfortingly real metal knob.

"I shall stand here until you return," the nun said coldly. "And hurry up. There are girls here trying to go to sleep."

The cloudy bathroom mirror reflected Daphne's frightened face back at her. "Am I going mad? I had them on when I got out of bed," she muttered feverishly, staring down at her bare legs. But she didn't dare take too long, so, after a few minutes, she made her way unsteadily back to the dorm.

"If everyone is quite ready now," Pauline Emmanuel hissed, as she shut the door behind her with a sharp click.

Lying stiffly in bed, Daphne reached down to touch a knee. But, heavens, what was this? The stockings *were* there. She could feel them as clearly as if she could see every silken stitch. *I am going mad*, she thought in a whirling panic.

By now the dormitory was quiet except for a few snores. Daphne swung her legs over the edge of the mattress.

No! It couldn't be true. It just couldn't. Standing in a pool of moonlight, Daphne watched in disbelief as the stockings changed gradually back to their original scarlet. Shocked, she returned to bed and clutched the covers up under her chin.

Too scared to sleep, she tried a hundred ways of explaining to herself what she'd just seen with her own eyes. At last, she found herself remembering something she'd once read in a Sherlock Holmes mystery. What was it the brilliant detective had said exactly?

"When you have considered all the facts and eliminated all the possibilities, however strange, that which remains, however improbable, must be the truth."

As the clock in St. Jude's bell tower struck three Daphne reached her own conclusion. Only one possibility remained.

The stockings must be magic.

Chapter Three

Daphne ran, sobbing with terror, across a huge shadowy stage, her scarlet ballet dress swirling around her. The snouted demon on her heels snarled and snapped in grim triumph, reaching out its fierce claws to catch her and tear her to pieces. Above the stage, thunder roared and lightning cracked across the lurid midnight sky.

Now she was climbing, trying to catch her breath, desperately reaching out for safety on the high ground above her. Far below stretched a gaping chasm, its wide edges lined with stunted, pointed trees. To her terrified gaze they looked like rotten teeth in the mouth of an ancient hag. Behind her she smelled the stinking breath of her pursuer. With a last despairing gasp, she hurled herself into space. And fell, sickeningly, endlessly downwards, into the lightless nothingness of the abyss.

In the next bed, Felicity shot up, startled. "DAPHNE, wake up!"

Daphne opened her eyes. She was drenched with

sweat; her heart was pounding so hard it felt as if it would explode.

"You were yelling your head off," Felicity said anxiously.

Daphne stretched and forced herself to say, as if it didn't matter, "Sorry. It was just a really horrible dream."

"As long as you're all right," Felicity replied, concerned.

Daphne's secrecy about anything important had become a habit. It wasn't that she didn't like Felicity. She did. Very much. She sat next to her in class and had the bed next to her in the dormitory, but she never let anyone, not Felicity, not even Sister Mary Euphoria, in on her deepest feelings. Trusting or loving people was much too dangerous. When she was little she'd believed with all her heart that her parents missed her and that one day they would come for her. Her presence at St. Jude's must be some kind of awful mistake.

As she got older, she realised the painful, bitter truth. Her parents didn't want her. They didn't miss her. And if they didn't care about her that must mean that she was a pathetic, unlovable nobody.

Her dreams of belonging somewhere, of being loved, perhaps of being talented and even famous, were nothing more than empty longings, an expensive luxury a penniless orphan couldn't afford. But there was one thing she could afford. Dignity. That meant keeping all her real feelings, all her pain and her loneliness, buried deep inside her. No one was going to pity her. Ever.

At breakfast Daphne was still wobbly. She was sure that horror of a dream had to be connected with the scarlet stockings. Had they really transformed themselves, or was that a part of her nightmare, too? Her throat was so tight she could hardly eat and, as soon as the meal was over, she hurried to the senior girls' bathroom and locked herself in a cubicle. With nervous fingers she took the stockings from the pocket of her uniform blazer. Quickly, she took off her shoes. Then she worked the scarlet stockings up over her grey cotton ones.

Straight away, the scarlet disappeared and a rippling wave of grey ran up her legs.

And everything Daphne had known so far turned crazily upside down.

Suddenly the parcel, the book, the riddle, the stockings, the dream, were all more than she could possibly cope with. *I've got to get them off,* she thought, panicking. She tore at the stockings, fearfully watching them return to scarlet, as she crammed them deep into the pocket of her blazer. Her stomach heaved and she was overcome by a wave of sickness. Just in time she managed to fling open the toilet lid.

As she fumbled for her handkerchief and wiped the perspiration from her forehead, the bell rang for her first class.

Morning lessons, lunch, and afternoon lessons went by in a blur. Still shaky and preoccupied, Daphne took her place in line beside Felicity for the daily afternoon walk. Wednesday's was Daphne's absolute favourite, because on Wednesday they always walked through Hoxton Market Square, home of the famous Britannia Theatre.

Two by two, the line of St. Jude's girls descended the red brick steps of the orphanage and set off, youngest girls in front, older girls behind. Sister Pauline Emmanuel was in her usual place at the head of the column; Sister Clare, the no-nonsense games mistress, brought up the rear.

Gradually the streets grew wider and more crowded. Then Hoxton Market Square burst gloriously into view. "Oh!" Daphne breathed, with a sigh of delight. She stood for a moment, drinking in the colourful, bustling scene in front of her. The sunlight danced down on the square's highest point, the stone figure of the mythical empress Britannia, seated regally in her chariot on a deep ledge high over the theatre's impressive entrance. The glittering rays turned to gold the statue's gilded, plumed helmet and the tip of her trident, held majestically aloft. Stone dolphins frolicked by Britannia's chariot while sea gods vigorously blew on their upraised conch shells. Proudly carved in stone just over the Britannia's main doors were the words

OPENED ON JUNE 18TH, 1858
BY HER MAJESTY, QUEEN VICTORIA.

The line of girls moved on, but Daphne lingered, wishfully. She'd never actually been inside the famous theatre, of course. St. Jude's couldn't afford tickets.

Hoxton was an ordinary working man's district which lay, centuries old, in the East End of London. It was because of the Brittania Theatre that Hoxton was famous. Audiences came from all over London to be thrilled by the array of stars who performed there. And, for almost a hundred years, the Britannia's Christmas Pantomime, with its magic and its slapstick comedy, had been the eagerly awaited annual treat of Hoxton's children. "No Panto for you this year if you don't be'ave," was the worst threat any Hoxton parent could utter.

"Stay together, girls," Sister Pauline Emmanuel barked. Happily, Daphne sniffed in the market's delicious smells of fruit, freshly baked bread and pies, and the perfume of thousands of flowers displayed in rows of buckets.

On a corner, Hoxton's only policeman, the stocky, red-cheeked Constable Bodger, stood knee-deep in children, all yelling "Me please, me please." From the pockets of his dark blue uniform with its polished silver buttons, the constable was making a performance of handing out gigantic round gobstoppers, guaranteed to provide hours of satisfaction. For his big finish, he swept off his helmet with a flourish and, from behind his ear, produced one last multicoloured sweet. He handed it over to a small boy with the smiling comment, "Orl right then, Patrick, you can 'ave it. I seen you carrying your Ma's shopping 'ome for 'er." Then he pretended to frown. "Now buzz off, the lot of you."

Looking backwards from her place in the line, Daphne smiled. This was what life *should* be like, full of fun.

Nearing the Britannia, she saw a crowd had gathered in front of the sweeping entrance steps. She could hear singing and the foot-tapping sound of an accordion. Her heart raced. No matter what happened, she absolutely had to find out exactly what was going on. With a glance ahead of her to establish the whereabouts of Sister Pauline Emmanuel, she slipped out of line. "Daphne DON'T, she'll kill you!" Felicity called urgently after her. But Daphne had already disappeared into the crowd.

There were three performers, two boys and a girl, all about Daphne's age, dancing and singing on the Britannia's wide bottom step. The song was a well-known old music-hall favourite called *My Old Man Said Follow the Van and Don't Dilly Dally On the Way*. The watching crowd roared out the chorus:

I dallied and I dillied
I dillied and I dallied
Lost me way and don't know where to roam.
Oh, there's no consolation like a London policeman
When you can't find your way 'ome.

Dressed in the wittiest costumes made of rags and patches in every colour imaginable, the trio was led by a very tall, very thin dark-haired boy. Next to him was a shorter, sturdier boy. *He's got the most wonderful voice and the nicest smile I've ever seen*, Daphne thought, staring entranced. The skinny girl was the one playing the accordion, her dark ginger curls tossing as she bent backwards and forwards, her fingers nimbly flying over the keys. *The Best of Friends*, the group's name, was handwritten in curlicues on a sign by their feet. Fascinated, Daphne noticed that, next to the sign, lay a battered brown velvet hat with a floppy pink rose, holding a few coppers.

The chorus came round again. *I know this song*, Daphne realised happily. *Sister Mary Euphoria taught it to us.* She joined in, adoring being a part of the crowd.

Too soon the performance ended. Coins rained into the hat. Daphne's ears rang with the applause. She clapped until her own palms stung. The shorter boy's eyes met hers and, beaming, he yelled out, "Glad you liked us!"

Suddenly, someone grabbed Daphne's elbow and roughly whirled her around.

"Were you SPEAKING to that boy? How DARE you remove yourself from the line? What were your instructions?" Sister Pauline Emmanuel shouted, her face red.

"Stay together," Daphne said, embarrassed. People all around her were staring. Her brief, shining happiness was gone. She shrank back into herself. *There's no point in trying to explain to her*, she thought, miserably.

"I'm warning you," Sister Pauline Emmanuel hissed. "You've been even more trouble than usual since you got that book of yours. Any further breaking of the rules and that will be the last you're going to see of *that* silly thing."

No, she wouldn't, she couldn't, Daphne thought angrily. With a final, longing glance behind her, she followed the nun back through the crowd. As she rejoined the line turning towards St Jude's, Felicity and some of the other girls gave her sympathetic looks. But it didn't help. Daphne still felt miserable.

She cheered up only when she passed the most colourful stall in the whole market.

GREEN'S FRUIT & VEG.
THREE GENERATIONS OF
FINEST PRODUCE.
Proprietors Carlo and Maria Green.

Daphne admired the beautiful display; the graceful piles of perfect tangerines and pink-flushed apples, the bursting sacks of walnuts and almonds and the fat Brussels sprouts laid out like oversized green pearl necklaces.

Green's was crowded, as usual. Behind the counter,

a middle-aged couple efficiently sold and wrapped, joking and gossiping with their customers. The woman was plump and wore her dark hair in an untidy knot, strands of which kept falling out of the bright combs that held it on top of her head. Today she wore a white-and-yellow-striped cotton dress, and, over it, a sky blue cardigan and a pink and green flowery apron. Avidly, Daphne drank in all the colours, a universe away from her own drab clothing.

"Where's your Joe today? I miss 'is lovely singing on the stall," a customer asked, loading her shopping bag.

"Over at the Britannia again, busy neglecting the family business for show business, I reckon 'ee is, Mrs. Langton," came the laughing reply from the man serving her. His tousled light brown hair showed streaks of grey and laugh lines crinkled around his smiling blue eyes. Always alert for details to fuel her imagination about the real world outside St. Jude's, Daphne noted that today he was wearing a deep blue shirt rolled up over his strong arms. *He must get those muscles from hefting crates around the place*, she thought. Seeing her watching, Carlo Green picked up four oranges and solemnly juggled them. Daphne beamed at him. But the other girls were right on her heels, and so, reluctantly, she had to move on.

If she could have stayed a few minutes longer, she would have heard something of extraordinary interest.

"Poor mites," Maria Green said. She and her husband looked sorrowfully after the drab departing line. "Carlo, 'ow are we ever going to choose?"

Her husband sighed. "Dunno, luv."

Chapter Four

"No, there's still been no decision, Daphne. I think you should try your best to stop thinking about it so much," Sister Mary Euphoria advised as she moved briskly through the room, sorting out choir sheet music. "It's going to flatten you if you aren't the one who's picked." Daphne longed to keep fishing for information, but she knew Sister Mary E. was talking sense. After all, she told herself, it wasn't as if she didn't have enough to think about. Like the scarlet stockings. As the days had passed, Daphne's panic about their unexplainable powers had begun to recede, replaced by the electric thrill she'd felt when she first held them in her hands. Whenever she could find a few minutes to herself, she tried them on, just to see if the magic, if it really was magic, was still working.

And, yes. The stockings still changed colour to match whatever was covering her legs. Every time it made her shiver. But that was *all* they did. Daphne was impressed, but, after she'd watched them do it over and over, she was starting to feel disappointed. She began to wonder whether it was no more than some sort of party trick. Yet the stockings and the book arrived together, she reasoned, and there was the matter of the riddle. Whatever could *First, you must find me* mean?

She'd spent days searching every inch of every room she could get into. But she had discovered nothing even vaguely mysterious. What if the clue was hidden somewhere she wasn't allowed to look, like the Mother Superior's office, or not in St. Jude's at all? For the first time, she felt discouraged. She was glad when Wednesday came round again. *Hoxton Market's just the sort of busy place where I might find the first clue*, she thought hopefully.

But, when the girls from St. Jude's got to the Market, Daphne noticed fewer people walking around than usual. Then she saw a huge crowd in front of the Britannia. Jumping up and down on the spot, Daphne managed to see over the rows of heads.

She turned to Felicity. "It's the cancan! They're all dressed as French dancing girls, even the boys!"

Felicity giggled. "Don't they look ridiculous?"

"No, they look funny and sweet!" she answered. "They're all made up with bright red lipstick and turquoise eyeshadow. *Ooh!* And they're wearing pink dresses with big swirly skirts, and frilly white bloomers and hats with feathers!"

Just then, the man and woman from Daphne's favourite market stall, Green's Fruit and Veg, dashed up. Carlo gave a piercing wolf whistle. "It's our Joe!" he told everyone around him, as the music got louder and louder. Moving quickly through the crowd, the couple worked their way right to the front.

Afterwards, Daphne could never explain why she did what she did. For a moment, everything but the cancan, even the book and the scarlet stockings, went completely out of her head. With a rush of joy, she flew through the crowd and up the Britannia's steps.

"Ooh la, la!" cried the two boys as they made a place for her between them. Laughing, feeling tipsy on the gaiety of the music and the cheers of the audience, Daphne joined in, kicking her legs up until her knees touched her nose. When she managed to get her leg straight up over her head, the other performers stood back admiringly to give her a solo of her own.

Among the applause and the laughter there came a berserk screeching noise like a warthog having a nervous breakdown. Sister Pauline Emmanuel charged up the steps. "YOU WICKED, WICKED GIRL!" she screamed. Drawing back her arm, she slapped Daphne hard across the face. As Daphne flinched, the accordion wheezed to a shocked halt. The crowd fell silent.

The nun elbowed the two boys aside and thrust her furious flushed face right into Daphne's. "You're a disgrace to St. Jude's," she shouted. "You were kicking your legs so high people could see your UNDERGARMENTS!" Roughly twisting Daphne's arm behind her back, the nun marched her down the steps. The crowd parted, staring and whispering as Sister Pauline Emmanuel dragged Daphne away.

"That poor kid, there was no need to humiliate 'er," Carlo said angrily, watching the pair disappear around a corner. "She wasn't 'urting nobody. She was just 'aving a bit of fun."

Maria dabbed at her eyes. "I can't abide cruelty. The way that old woman slapped 'er and dragged 'er off, you'd 'ave thought the girl was a criminal."

Daphne suddenly found her voice in the doorway of St. Jude's. A lifetime of pent-up grief, rage and frustration erupted. "I won't be a dreary NOBODY like you!" she shouted at Pauline Emmanuel. "I've got ambition and guts, more than you've ever had in your miserable, jealous, pathetic life."

Pushing her way past the dumbfounded nun, Daphne

31

flew up the stairs. She ran into the dormitory and flung herself onto her bed, her whole body shaking with harsh tears. Blindly, she groped for the book and the scarlet stockings and clutched them fiercely to her. *I suppose that vile old witch is going to come up now and take these away from me*, she thought.

But no one came, not even Sister Mary Euphoria, the only person Daphne could have borne to talk to. Several hours went by as she lay curled up, cold and miserable, in the dark. Then, as the clock in the bell tower chimed eight, Daphne heard the sound of quick, light footsteps. Her bedside lamp clicked on. Blinking in the sudden glare, she saw, with relief, it was Sister Mary Euphoria.

"Stop crying," the nun said gently, sitting down and handing Daphne a starched handkerchief from her pocket. "It's going to be all right. They've come to collect you."

Daphne's whole body tensed. Here it came. The trouble she knew she was in. She clenched her fingers over the handkerchief. "Who's come? Is Mother Superior sending me away?"

"Oh, my poor child, *no*. Your new family's come to collect you."

Daphne shot upright. "What? They chose ME?"

Sister Mary Euphoria gave a huge grin. "Hurry up and come downstairs. Mr. and Mrs. Green and their son, Joe, are waiting for you in the visitors' room." She peered at Daphne. "I think it might be a good idea, though, to splash some cold water on your face and brush your hair. You don't want to frighten them to death!"

Daphne was having difficulty taking in what Sister Mary Euphoria had said. Could it really be that the moment she'd been waiting for all her life had finally arrived? And just when she'd been in the depths of despair! She leapt off the bed with a yell and pulled the laughing young nun into a mad galloping dance around the dormitory.

Suddenly, Daphne froze, her face flushing a dull red. "Oh, *no!*" she cried. "Mr. and Mrs. Green, from Green's Fruit and Veg? I saw them at the Britannia today. How horribly, dreadfully embarrassing."

"Be glad they were there, Daphne," said Sister Mary Euphoria. "They were approved to adopt weeks ago, but they've been dithering over their choice. Apparently it was their son who helped them to make up their minds this afternoon."

"Mr. Green shouted out that his Joe was one of The Best of Friends," Daphne said excitedly. "Which one do you think was Joe? The handsome, tall one or the one with the wonderful singing voice and the big grin?"

"You're going to find out in a few minutes," Sister Mary Euphoria replied affectionately. "Off you go. Wash your face and brush your hair."

Daphne shook her head in wonder. "I can't believe they really want me." She hurried off to the bathroom to make herself presentable.

"I suppose I shouldn't really be telling you this," Mary Euphoria said a few minutes later, as she accompanied Daphne down the stairs. "But the Reverend Mother isn't very pleased with Sister Pauline after what happened today. I just thought you'd like to know."

Daphne felt unreal. Everything was changing so quickly she couldn't quite keep up with it all. It was Sister Pauline who was in trouble, not her! The Greens were waiting to take her home! She came to a shaky stop and turned to Sister Mary Euphoria. "Thank you for being on my side," she said quietly. "You've always tried to make me feel as if I was worth caring about."

The nun gazed intently into Daphne's eyes. "Of course you are, Daphne. You must always remember and believe that."

"I'll try," Daphne said. But secretly she longed to admit that, now that somebody actually wanted her,

34

she was so terrified she didn't want to go. What if the Greens didn't like her? Could they send her back to St. Jude's? But those fears, rising from the deepest part of her, remained unspoken. For her survival, she'd built a wall around her feelings. She didn't dare allow that wall to show so much as a chink, not even to Sister Mary Euphoria.

Outside the closed door of the visitors' room, Daphne trembled with nerves. She shut her eyes and took several ragged breaths.

"Don't worry," Mary Euphoria said. "They'll love you!"

Chapter Five

The delicious smell of bacon frying crept under the door of Daphne's new bedroom and woke her. She stretched, for a blank second not knowing where she was. But then the memory of her warm welcome to 52 Upper, Market Square the night before rushed happily back.

"I 'ope you like yellow, love," Maria Green had said anxiously as she'd opened the bedroom door. "And flowers, 'cos there's a lot of 'em in 'ere on your curtains and bedspread."

Daphne had stood silently, drinking it all in. "It's more beautiful than I could even imagine, Mrs. Green," she'd breathed.

Maria's good-natured face had flushed with pleasure. This was just the reaction she'd hoped for when she was stitching the quilted coverlet, and putting frills on the cushions for the white wicker armchair by the window with its view across to the Britannia. And all for a girl she'd never met.

"Just call us Carlo and Maria, luv," she'd said, tactfully. "Till you feel comfortable with Mum and Dad."

Now, as the morning sun streamed in, Daphne heard a knock at the door, and a voice called, "All right to come in?"

"Yes, do," Daphne called back, stretching luxuriously again under the softest sheets and warmest blankets she'd ever felt.

Joe Green appeared in the doorway. "I don't suppose you're hungry at all!" Before Daphne could admit she was absolutely starving, the front doorbell pealed. "We've got guests for breakfast," Joe said, going off to answer it.

"My old man said follow the van and don't dilly dally on the way," Daphne sang happily. She jumped out of bed and flung open the white painted door of her wardrobe, where her St Jude's uniform was hanging. Today, even the sight of that depressing grey dress couldn't take the smile off her face.

Before leaving the room, Daphne opened her bedside drawer to make sure that *How to Teach Yourself Ballet* and the scarlet stockings were safely inside, where she'd put them. She pulled out the book and opened it for another quick look at the riddle. *I don't suppose* **First, you must find me** *means the Green family, does it?* She tried to work it out logically. *Because really they found me if I'm meant to be very specific.*

Suddenly feeling awkward, she dawdled down the long corridor outside her bedroom to the kitchen. Taking a deep breath, she opened the door to the sunny room. It seemed to be full of people.

"Morning, gel," Carlo said, looking up from the *Hoxton Daily Gazette.* "Sleep well?"

"Yes, thank you Mr. Green. Sorry, I mean Carlo," Daphne blushed, hovering in the doorway. Maria beamed at her from the stove, where she was busy with a bowl of eggs and a frying pan.

Joe got up from his seat at the well-worn wooden table. "Let me introduce you to the others in Hoxton's own destined-for-certain-stardom group, The Best of Friends," he announced with a flourish. "Daphne, may I present Roland Spires and Dolly Cheadle."

"Call me Lofty," the tall, dark-haired boy said, a shy smile lighting up his handsome face.

"What an appalling dress!" said the slender red-haired girl who had played the accordion. She beamed at Daphne. "Here, sit next to me." She indicated the empty chair. "Have some toast and marmalade."

Feeling very self-conscious, Daphne sat.

"Suppose she doesn't like marmalade, Bossyboots!"

Joe said to Dolly. He turned to Daphne. "She can't help it, poor thing. Comes of being the oldest of five sisters. And what a temper! None of them want to get on the wrong side of her!"

"It's a good job for The Best of Friends there's someone around to organise you two sorry objects!" Dolly retorted.

"Would you rather have strawberry jam than marmalade?" Lofty asked quietly.

Daphne felt grateful to him for noticing that she was overwhelmed. She wasn't used to choices.

"Yes, what would you like, luv? We've got bacon and sausages and eggs," Maria called out from the stove.

"And mushrooms and tomatoes from the stall. Bet you've never tasted nothing like them, s'right Joe?" Carlo asked proudly.

"S'right, Pa." Joe sat down to finish mopping up the egg left on his blue-and-white-spotted plate.

Without waiting for a politely proper answer, Maria set down a heaped plate in front of Daphne. "Tuck in, luv. You're a Green now. We've got to fatten you up a bit," Carlo teased. "You can't 'elp on the stall looking like a ghost. Shocking for business that'd be!"

Was it only yesterday that she'd walked past Green's

Fruit and Veg, a complete stranger to this kind family? "When can I help you in the Market, Carlo?" she asked eagerly.

"Not this morning, I hope." Dolly said as she helped herself to another cup of tea. "I thought we might go back to my house after breakfast, Daphne, so I can measure you up for some new clothes. My Dad's got the haberdashery stall in the market next to the Greens," she continued. "Ma's a dressmaker on the side, so she's got stacks of leftover material. And, after I get your measurements, I've got your Girls' Independent School uniform for you to try on. It'll need alterations before term starts again after Easter. Everything will be too big though. It used to belong to the daughter of a friend of Maria's called Ethel. She's a giantess."

"Ethel's a giantess, not Maria's friend!" Lofty explained helpfully.

Of course, there'll be a new school, Daphne realised with a mixture of elation and terror. Elation, because there might be dance classes at Girls' Independent. Terror, because, what if she couldn't keep up? What if they despised her because she was the only one in the whole place who was an orphan from St. Jude's? That was too awful to think about. She didn't want to spoil her perfect breakfast, so, as usual she kept her fears to herself. "Dolly, it's incredibly nice of you to want to make me some things to wear. Thank you so much," Daphne said. Then she realised. "You can sew! All sorts of things, probably. Did you make those wonderful cancan costumes?"

"Dolly makes all our costumes, and our props, too," Lofty said. "Bossy but talented, aren't you, Doll?"

"Yep, she's Miss Make and Mend," Joe put in. "Learned carpentry and repairs from her dad and sewing from her mum."

"And she learned the accordion from her grandfather. He used to be the pianist in the Britannia's orchestra," Lofty added.

"Did you invent that cage I saw last week with the bird that fell off its perch?" Daphne asked.

Dolly nodded. "I did," she said, matter-of-factly.

"It was fantastic, so funny the way it went all droopy and just flopped down! How on earth did you think of it?"

"Don't know, really," Dolly said, through a mouthful of toast. "I sit down with a pencil and a sketch pad and the ideas seem to come."

"She's training herself to be a set and costume designer. We're nothing but her human mannequins!" Joe said solemnly.

"I wish you were, then you wouldn't be able to talk the amazing rubbish you do!" Dolly retorted, glaring at him in mock fury.

"Do you mind if I ask how old you are?" Daphne asked, wishing she had even a tenth of their self-confidence. "You're all so brilliant. We were a very quiet lot at St. Jude's."

"We're all fourteen," Joe answered. "And wait till Dolly's finished with you, you won't recognise yourself!"

"Not too gussied up please. Or else I'll 'ave to 'ave a word with your Ma, Dolly," Maria said, only half joking. "Dolly's mother and me 'ave been friends for a long time," she explained to Daphne. "Made my wedding dress, didn't she, Doll?"

"Yes, Mrs. G," Dolly said. Then she gave Daphne a knowing look. "Keep an eye on Joe, though, Daphne. He's bound to overact his new brother role. Insisting on knowing where you're going and when you'll be back, things like that." She leaned over, smiling, and gave Joe a big poke in the ribs.

"Ouch! Now who's talking rubbish?" Joe beamed back at her.

Daphne's eyes shone. She loved all of it, the jokes and the feeling of fun and affection in the kitchen. "How did The Best of Friends begin?" she asked.

Maria interrupted firmly. "Daphne, stop talking and start eating, luv. Before it orl goes cold."

Daphne tucked in. "Maria, this is the most delicious food I've had in my whole life. I mean it," she said a few appreciative minutes later. "I hope I won't be a nuisance if I haunt you in the kitchen to find out how you do everything!"

Maria's face turned pink with pleasure. "We can start whenever you want, luv." She clattered some saucepans around. "Don't want to waste yer Easter 'olidays sitting 'ere though, do you?" she asked cheerfully.

"No, we don't, Ma," Joe agreed with a grin.

"Get a move on then, the lot of you." Carlo said. "I'm off to open the stall. Be along this afternoon to help will you, Joe and Daphne?"

"Oh, yes, please Carlo, if I won't be in the way," Daphne said eagerly.

He smiled at her. "Luverly to 'ave another pair of 'ands."

To Daphne's delight, Joe grabbed her arm and swept her out of the kitchen with the others. They clattered down the stairs from No. 52 Upper and out into the market square. "You were going to tell me how The Best of Friends started," Daphne reminded him. She smiled as she raised her face to the early morning warmth of the sun.

Lofty put his hand on his heart and bowed. "Please be so good as to accompany us to our stage." They crossed the square and sat down on the imposing flight of steps in front of the Britannia's main entrance.

"It was Lofty's idea," Joe explained. "When he was growing up he came to the Britannia's Pantos every Christmas, and he got stage-struck, just like I did. And Doll practically lived at the theatre, watching her grandfather's rehearsals. Anyway, Lofty came to Green's to do some shopping for his ma, about a year ago, and there I was, singing my lungs out for the customers."

"A thunderbolt suddenly hit me at the same time Joe hit high C!" Lofty explained.

"Later he came back and said he'd been thinking we could work up some kind of an act to do in the market," Joe went on. "You know, our own versions of the music hall songs and Panto comedy routines the Britannia does. So then I said I knew just the right person to do us some bang-up costumes, and we went to see Dolly. And she said yes, and that she'd play the accordion as well, and dance and sing a bit. Then, when we were thinking what to call ourselves, Lofty came up with The Best of Friends, because by that time, we were."

"Look at those dramatic cheekbones and that romantically tousled hair. He's going to be the finest actor of his generation, aren't you Lofty?" Dolly teased.

"Every time I read something I like it's as though I can feel the words leaping off the page and into my head, begging to be spoken out loud," Lofty said seriously. " It takes me ages to get through a book."

Daphne was bursting with questions. "Why are you called Lofty when your real name's Roland?"

"Joke," Joe explained. "He's called Spires. And he's so tall. Lofty Spires. Get it?"

Lofty's face lit up. "Listen everyone, I think I've had a truly good idea for a new show. I bet we could make it the biggest hit we've ever had, with Dolly's costuming genius, Joe's famous singing, and my limited acting ability." He stopped abruptly, seeing Daphne's wistful face. His kind heart interpreted her expression correctly. He looked over, questioningly, at Joe and Dolly. They both nodded back.

"Only thing is, we haven't got a really first-class dancer," Lofty said. "Any interest, Daphne?"

Daphne couldn't believe her ears! "Any interest! Could I really, Lofty? I've never had any proper training, but I've been dancing ever since I was tiny and recently someone sent me a book that's been a big help."

"We all admired your audition piece. Finest interpretation of the cancan I've ever seen!" Lofty said firmly. "Anyone got a pencil on them?"

Dolly reached into her handbag and pulled out a paintbrush. "No, but will this do?"

Solemnly, Lofty motioned Daphne to her feet.

"Rise, all Friends," he intoned. "Stand forth, Daphne Green." Daphne held her breath as Lofty tapped her on each shoulder with the brush and declaimed, "By the gods of music, by the gods of dance, by the gods of tragedy and by the gods of comedy, I declare you officially from this day forth and eternally a Friend."

Daphne's knees went wobbly, she couldn't even reply. *Do these nice, talented people really want me for a friend, really want me to be in the Friends*, she marvelled. *From today onwards dancing won't make me weird or different, it'll make me a part of something wonderful!*

"I'll tell you what we're going to do," Dolly said. "First, Daphne, we'll go to my house and measure you up for some skirts and dresses and blouses and a coat."

"Then, when you've quite finished monopolising her, Doll," Lofty interjected, "we'll all go to my house. We'll need my father's encyclopaedias for what I've got in mind."

There was a sudden flurry of activity behind them.

They all turned to watch as two men in overalls appeared carrying buckets and long-handled brushes.

"Hey!" Joe said. "Something big must be coming to the Britannia." The Friends stared as the workmen pasted huge banners into place:

THE WORLD FAMOUS BALLET
SPLENDIDE DE PARIS

**ON TOUR IN THEIR ACCLAIMED PRODUCTION
OF SWAN LAKE.
STARRING PRIMA BALLERINA ASSOLUTA,
OVA ANDOVA
AS ODETTE/ODILE**

"It's *her*!" Daphne cried out.

"Who's *her*?" Joe asked.

"Madame Ova Andova. She's absolutely the most famous ballet star in the world, even more famous than Anna Pavlova. All the other great dancers are called prima ballerinas. She's the only one who's allowed to call herself a prima ballerina *assoluta*. I worship her. In this ballet they're doing, *Swan Lake*, the star has to dance two characters. One's called Odette and she's wonderful. The other one's horrible. She's called Odile.

It's supposed to be amazingly difficult to do it properly," Daphne explained. "Sister Mary Euphoria used to collect every newspaper clipping about Madame Andova she could find for me. You can't imagine how fantastic she is."

They gazed at the huge photographs. One of them showed Andova as Odette, fragile and beautiful, dressed in floating white, with a headdress of soft white feathers circling her shining dark hair. In the next she was the evil Odile, dressed in the colour of a midnight sky and drenched in diamonds, her mouth set in a cruel smile. Daphne felt she could stand there forever, but then Joe tapped her on the shoulder, saying, "Come back to earth, Daphne, you can worship at Andova's shrine later!"

With a last long look, Daphne tore herself away and they all set off for Dolly's house through Hoxton's narrow streets. The roads teemed with pushcarts, bicycles and horse-drawn delivery vans. Daphne stared around her, wishing she had at least two more pairs of eyes and ears so she could absorb it all.

"We're not up to date here like they are in the middle of London, worse luck," Lofty said. "We still don't get many automobiles, and when we do, the kids make a nuisance of themselves trailing after 'em."

"Lofty's Dad, Doctor Spires, has got one, though," Dolly chimed in, seeing Lofty was too modest to mention it himself. "Right posh, aren't you me old ducks?" she asked with an impish grin.

"I'm not posh," Lofty said, embarrassed. "I go to Hoxton Boys' Grammar, just like Joe."

"Yes, but I'm only a scholarship boy," Joe said with mock humbleness.

"That's much better than just having parents who can luckily afford to send you. You got in because of your talent," Lofty replied seriously, his hand on Joe's shoulder.

Dolly nodded. "Joe is a huge part of why Green's is so popular," she explained. "He sings for the customers while they're waiting to be served. And one day the Headmaster of Hoxton Grammar came along to buy some veg, and Mr. Green came right out and asked him if he'd consider giving Joe a scholarship so that he could go to a school with a first-class singing teacher."

"All right," Joe said, red-faced. "Don't bore her to death!"

Daphne wanted to hold on to every moment of that day, but all too soon it rushed past her. By eight o'clock she could hardly keep her eyes open, and Maria said she'd better have an early night.

With a sleepy "goodnight," Daphne left the Greens in the front parlour sitting on a vast squashy sofa upholstered in worn yellow velvet. "We've had this sofa ever since I can remember," Joe had explained to Daphne. "We call it the Plonkit, because you plonk down into it."

Once Daphne's bedroom door had shut, Joe explained his brilliant idea to welcome her to the family.

After he'd finished, Maria looked excited and Carlo said approvingly, "I'll 'ave a word tomorrow with me old mate, Tom."

Chapter Six

Daphne felt as if she had balloons tied to her wrists that would float her right up to the Britannia's golden, cloud-painted ceiling. With a sigh of bliss, she opened her programme to the title page and read, '*Swan Lake*, Starring Ova Andova'.

Joe nudged her and motioned towards his father, sitting, fidgeting, on Daphne's other side. Carlo saw them grinning at him and declared in martyred tones, "I've never been 'ere for anything like this!" he told Daphne. "Only for you, gel, would I get dressed up like a dog's dinner to watch a bunch of fancy toffs prancing around doing ballet. One-time-only offer, this is, far as I'm concerned!"

From their seats in the topmost of the Britannia's three balconies Daphne and Joe, Carlo and Maria looked down over the crowded theatre. Below, in the expensive orchestra seats, the sparkle of jewels and the crisp white of the men's evening dress shirts announced the presence of fashionable London. Excited chatter filled the huge auditorium.

"Good old Britannia," Carlo said proudly. "They come to 'Oxton from all over for our shows."

"Tonight it's because of Madame Andova," Daphne said, her eyes shining. This all seemed like a dream. In a few moments she'd actually be seeing her idol dance!

The crystal chandeliers dimmed until the theatre was dark. The rustling of programmes and an occasional cough were the only sounds to be heard. The lights in the orchestra pit flashed on as the silver-haired conductor entered and stood smiling and bowing to the applause.

Turning to the musicians, he raised his baton. The first notes of the composer Tchaikovsky's romantic overture filled the auditorium with an otherworldly sound. As the footlights glowed pink and amber, the cherry-red velvet curtains swept apart and Daphne felt she was being pulled with them, into a world of enchantment.

She'd imagined thousands of times what a real ballet would be like, but nothing she'd dreamed of came close to this reality, sparkling in front of her inside the stage's golden frame.

Spellbound, Daphne watched as the Prince tried to choose a bride from among the aristocratic girls assembled in the palace ballroom for him by his mother, the Queen. In a series of dazzling duets, he partnered each would-be princess as they competed to win his heart.

Daphne leaned forward, her face in her hands, lost in the astounding grace and power of the dancers, the fairy-tale beauty of the sets and costumes, the melting colours of the stage lighting, and the sweeping music.

Carlo and Maria's eyes met Joe's smilingly. "Good idea, lad!" Carlo mouthed to his son behind Daphne's back.

Onstage, the scene changed. Daphne held her breath because she knew what would happen next.

In the woods by a lake the Prince, armed with a bow and arrow for hunting, watched a trio of beautiful swans gliding across the water and out of sight. Daphne grabbed Joe's arm and held on hard, because suddenly there *she* was — Odette, the Swan Princess, the famous prima ballerina *assoluta* herself, the great Russian dancer, Ova Andova.

Daphne's heart lurched as the Prince swept Andova up and held her tenderly by her slender waist, her head almost touching the floor, her legs in their satin ballet shoes held high in a graceful line behind her. She looked impossibly light, as if a puff of air would blow her away. Seconds later, she was spinning and leaping with all the flexible strength of fine wire, performing each seemingly impossible movement as if it was so easy anyone could do it if they tried.

The intermission came all too soon. Daphne stayed, glued to her seat, gazing around her in case she might miss anything. The musicians disappeared under the stage. Thuds and bangs came from behind the curtains. *I expect that's the scenery being changed*, she thought. *I wonder how they do it so quickly.*

In what seemed like only moments, the interval was over and Act 2 began.

Andova's spectacular dancing as the evil enchantress, Odile, cast its spell over the entire audience. And even though Daphne wished it would go on forever, *Swan Lake,* with its haunting message of the power of love over death and time, came to an end. As the curtains swept together, the applause thundered into a standing ovation. Eyes squeezed tightly shut, Daphne made a solemn vow. "One day I'll dance on the same stage as Andova, I swear it." Then, she jumped to her feet, clapping until her palms hurt.

The stage lights brightened and the prima ballerina *assoluta*, head modestly bent, stepped out in front of the velvet curtains to take her solo bows. With one graceful hand she touched her heart and then her lips. She took two or three of the brilliant red roses from the bouquet in her arms and, smiling, tossed them out into the cheering audience.

Then the house lights came up, leaving Daphne stranded somewhere between an enchanted lake and plain old everyday Hoxton. "Come on then, luv," Carlo said, steering her towards an exit. "'Ow would you like to go backstage?"

"Can we really, Carlo?"

"Yep, we're off to meet my old china, Tom," Carlo replied.

Daphne was completely baffled. "Old China? What do you mean, Carlo?"

"Rhyming slang for *mate*. China plate. Mate. Tom's the Britannia's stage doorman," Carlo explained. "We've known each other since we was kids. Me and 'im 'ad the desks next to each other in school. Proper couple of lads, we was. Course, that was an 'undred years ago now." He nudged Daphne, jokingly.

They left the theatre and walked down a narrow alley, which led to a plain entrance painted with the words, **STAGE DOOR**. Pausing, Daphne reached out and touched the printed letters just to make sure they were real.

In his cubicle just inside the door, Tom greeted them with a smile. "Seats orl right, then?" he asked.

"You done us proud, mate," Carlo said, shaking Tom's hand vigorously.

Tom's clear eyes surveyed Daphne. "'Eard you was living with the Greens now. Not a bad bunch, are they, once you get to know 'em?" he asked solemnly.

Almost speechless with excitement, Daphne managed to reply suitably and politely, all the while avidly scrutinising a real, live stage doorkeeper. Tom was thin and wiry. His hair was dark, except for a few threads of grey. He wore checked trousers, a knitted bottle green waistcoat and a white shirt. His wire spectacles perched on the end of his beaky nose.

To Daphne's delight, the Ballet Splendide company began to stream past Tom's desk, calling out "Bonsoir, goodnight." Even dressed in ordinary street clothes, they looked extraordinarily glamorous.

"'Ere, Bert!" Tom said, beckoning to a spotty lad of about sixteen. "Take Daphne and show 'er the stage." To Daphne he said, "Bert's our call-boy. It's 'is job to go round the dressing rooms fifteen minutes before the curtain goes up to tell the performers 'ow long they've got before they go on-stage."

In a semi-daze Daphne followed the boy through the

black-painted wings and out onto the stage. The huge auditorium was empty except for a few cleaning ladies, with scarves wrapped like turbans around their heads, gossiping and cackling with laughter as they swept among the seats.

Daphne decided to make her dream of dancing on the same stage as Andova come true immediately. Tentatively, she took her first few thrilling steps.

Suddenly, a loud voice from somewhere overhead shouted "Oi, you. Git on out of it. Lights going orf." Daphne froze. The call-boy, who hadn't spoken a single word to her in all this time, now jerked his head at her and took her back to the stage door.

The Greens and Tom were still deep in conversation. Daphne stared at a metal staircase, wondering where it led.

"Grushka," an attractively foreign musical voice rang out from above, "Where am I meeting his Excellency for dinner? The Ritz, no?"

A gruff voice answered. "Yes, Ovushka. This is why I am putting out your new evening dress."

Daphne felt her heart race because, surely, that delicious voice talking about 'His Excellency' could only belong to one person!

First of all, a wonderful smell, like bluebells in a

wood in spring, wafted down the staircase. Drinking it in, Daphne remembered a newspaper clipping describing exactly this exquisite fragrance called Ova, created especially for the star by the famous French designer, Poiret.

Light, quick footsteps rang out on the iron steps. High-heeled black suede shoes with diamond buckles appeared, then beautiful legs clad in sheer silk stockings, followed by the hem of a silver dress glittering with pearly lace. And finally, the head and shoulders of the dazzling Andova herself. Her exquisite face was framed by a little velvet hat with a veil sprinkled with what looked like stardust. A thick silver fox fur dropped casually from one slender shoulder.

Behind the ballerina lumbered a clunky bear of an old woman, dressed in black from head to toe, with a patterned shawl tied around her head. The Grushka referred to, Daphne presumed. This person carried a large red crocodile-skin make-up case with gold handles and the initials 'O.A.' picked out in diamonds and rubies.

Daphne, reduced almost to jelly with adoration, pulled herself together as Andova approached. With lowered eyes she dropped her idol an adoring curtsey.

Suddenly she had a fantastic thought. *What if Madame Andova is really my mother? After all, she's often*

danced in Rome where my mysterious package came from.
And her hair is exactly the same colour as mine!

Thrilled, Daphne felt soft fingers with red-tipped nails gently raising her face. "Charming!" the prima ballerina *assoluta* declared. With a goodnight nod to Tom, she swept out of the stage door to the chauffeured car that was waiting for her. Her dresser, Grushka, stomped along in her wake.

Daphne came down to earth with a bump.

"'Ow did you like the stage then, Daphne?" Tom asked, seemingly unaware that a goddess had just passed him by.

"I only saw it for a moment, but it was glorious, thank you," Daphne said faintly.

"Tell you what," Tom replied. "When the Splendide's run is finished, I'll show you round the 'ole place. Lots of 'istory in the old Britannia. I'll let you know when I can fix it up."

"Oh, yes please, Tom," Daphne said. "I'd love it more than anything."

With that, they all said goodnight and walked home across the square to 52 Upper.

Half asleep, Daphne was snuggled down in the Plonkit with a steaming cup of cocoa in her hand, when Maria handed her an envelope.

"What is it, Maria?" Daphne asked, surprised.

"Open it, you daft thing and you'll find out!" Joe said with one of his biggest grins.

Daphne tore at the envelope. Inside was a letter, signed by someone called Miss Cordelia Pettigrew, inviting Daphne to become a pupil at her Hoxton Ballet School, classes every Monday, Wednesday and Saturday from 4 to 7 p.m.

"Proper ballet lessons! At a proper ballet school! How can we possibly afford it?"

Carlo smiled. "Miss Pettigrew's a good customer. Don't you worry, gel. We've come to a satisfactory arrangement, Pettigrew and me."

Daphne grasped Carlo and Maria's hands in hers. Could people really be so kind?

"If I live to be a hundred, I'll never be able to thank you enough for this," she said passionately.

But she might not have been so thrilled if she'd known that the Pettigrew School of Ballet was going to make her unhappier than she'd ever been in her life before.

Chapter Seven

"Stand still!" Dolly mumbled, her mouth full of pins. She knelt in the Greens' sunny kitchen, fiddling with the hem of Daphne's almost-finished mint green linen skirt.

Maria, and Dolly's mother, Sheila Cheadle, watched from the table, a cup of mid-morning tea and a plate of chocolate biscuits in front of them. Maria knitted speedily away at the matching green cardigan she was making for Daphne.

Dolly finished pinning and stood back, her eyes narrowed in appraisal. Maria tutted. "Dolly, you're never going to send 'er out in that?"

"They wear 'em shorter now, Maria," Sheila said, brushing biscuit crumbs off her ample front.

"I've made a skirt just like it for me, Mrs. G," Dolly said, smiling.

"Got to keep up with the latest styles," Sheila Cheadle added, reassuringly.

Maria subsided. If the maker of Maria's wedding dress said it was all right, who was she to argue?

Daphne realised she'd better change the subject. Quickly. "Mrs. Cheadle," she said, "Dolly told me your telephone came yesterday. How exciting!"

The Cheadles were the first people in the market to install a telephone at home. "It did, luv," Sheila answered, "with an 'ole set of instructions called "Ow to Pass and Receive a Telephone Call'. When it rings you 'ave to take off the receiver and say your name at once. You're not supposed to say "Ullo' or "Oo's there?' Course, we don't expect to get many calls 'cos no one we know's on the phone. We got it just in case of emergency, like." She smiled with tolerant pride. "My 'Arry's always got to 'ave the latest thing!"

"Can Joe and I come and see it this evening?" Daphne asked. She looked down, imploringly. "Could you please get a move on, Dolly? I told Carlo I'd be down to help him on the stall as soon as you'd finished."

"You can't hurry perfection." Dolly said airily. "All right, you can hop down now."

Daphne got off the kitchen chair. "I love this skirt. You're so brilliant, Doll. If we're done, would you mind coming to my room with me while I change? I'll be quick."

When the kitchen door had closed behind the two girls, Mrs. Cheadle gave her friend a knowing look. "You don't 'ave to say nothing, Maria. You're like a different woman since that girl came 'ere."

"Honest, Sheila, I never thought I could be so 'appy," Maria replied. "When we lost our baby after we'd waited all them years to 'ave one, and Dr. Spires said we couldn't 'ave no more, I was so miserable I didn't want to think about kids ever again. It was our Joe 'oo talked us into adopting. And 'ee was right. She's so grateful for every little thing we do for 'er. Carlo's soppy about 'er already, thinks the sun shines out of 'er."

"I can see she's a nice girl, but 'Arry and me 'ave remarked she seems a bit standoffish at times. Shy, like."

"Thing is, Sheila, she's bin 'urt so bad, she don't really trust nobody," Maria explained earnestly. "You wouldn't believe some of the things she's told us. She said being an orphan makes you feel something's wrong with you that can't never be put right, like you must be 'orrible and unlovable."

Sheila tutted sympathetically. "Flippin' shame, that's what it is."

"Carlo said she might come to feel like a real daughter in time, Sheila, but I never thought it'd 'appen so quick. She's starved for affection and too afraid to show it, that's what I reckon. First day she was 'ere, she asked me to teach her 'ow to cook. Since then, she's been 'elping me every day. This morning she got up special and made Carlo's breakfast for 'im when it was still dark, before 'ee went off to our produce supplier. 'Ee usually makes do with a quick cuppa tea and 'as 'is breakfast on the run later. She made a good job of it, too. Pleased as a dog with three tails, Carlo was." Maria smiled proudly.

Down the hall, in Daphne's bedroom, Dolly was saying, "So this is the famous book that's teaching you ballet." She picked it up. "What's this handwriting?"

"That riddle, thing, you mean?" Daphne said, her old secretive self pretending not to be very interested.

"I love riddles." Dolly put the book down and flopped on the bed. "Oh, I've just remembered. Isn't this your first day at ballet school?"

"Yes, I've got to be at Miss Pettigrew's at four."

"Nervous?"

"Terrified. I've been practising my pliés all morning."

Quickly tying back her hair with a ribbon, Daphne said, "There, ready. Thanks for keeping me company."

"I'll pop round later to see how you got on. Good luck!" Dolly said.

* * *

Daphne ran out to the market. She found that Joe was at Green's Fruit and Veg with Carlo. "Dunno why," Carlo said, "but there's not bin much business today. The 'ole market's dead as a dodo. Reckon you two could manage on yer own while I take this veg up to Maria for tonight? Might stop and have a quick cuppa, too."

"Course, Dad," Joe said. "We'll try to make sure Green's doesn't go bankrupt while you're gone!"

"Mind you do, then!" Carlo said, giving his son a friendly nudge. Picking up a straw basket, loaded with vegetables and fruit, he sauntered off, whistling.

There was only one customer. While Joe served her, Daphne sat down on an upturned crate behind the stall. Talking to Dolly about the riddle had made her realise she'd rather let it slip during the last few days. "I'm sorry," she whispered. "I haven't forgotten about you."

She concentrated. *First, you must find me.* Find what? Perhaps it was something scarlet like the stockings? She picked up a shining ripe tomato and a red pepper and sat with them in her hands, as if waiting for them to say something. When they didn't after several minutes, she put them back, thinking disappointedly, *that's not the right answer to the clue, then.*

With a cheerful goodbye to the customer, Joe flopped

down beside her. "What was in your mind just then?" he asked. "You looked so serious."

"I'm afraid, Joe," Daphne blurted out. "I don't deserve to be this happy. I'm so worried something's bound to happen to take it all away, and then I'll be back at St. Jude's."

"You poor old thing, you mustn't think much of yourself, if you think you don't deserve to be happy."

"It's just that I've had to learn to look the facts in the face. The truth is my own mother and father didn't want me." Daphne fumbled for a handkerchief in the pocket of her apron. Head down, she blew her nose, shakily.

"Goodness, you have got yourself into a state," Joe said gently. "You don't know how you got to St. Jude's, so how do you know for sure no one wanted you? In any case, even if they didn't, that's not your fault. You were only a baby, so you couldn't have done anything wrong." He gave Daphne's shoulder a friendly squeeze. "And I'll tell you something else as well," he said firmly. "You can stop worrying about Mum and Dad ever sending you back to St. Jude's. You're a smash hit as a Green!"

Daphne smiled gratefully. "*Really*, Joe?"

"Yes, really my girl."

Daphne paused. "I'm so fond of you all. But please don't think I'm the most ungrateful person in the world if I say I still want to find my real parents. I never really stop thinking about it deep down. If I knew where I came from, I'd be able to find the bit of me that's missing. Do you understand what I mean?"

"Course I do," Joe said briskly. "I'd feel exactly the same way. And you wouldn't be hurting anyone's feelings if you told Carlo and Maria the same thing." With a final comforting pat, he jumped to his feet. "All right, curtain up. Two old trouts with big shopping baskets walking in our direction." He broke into glorious song, *"If you were the only girl in the world and I were the only boy.* That's right, ladies, this way. Three generations of finest produce!"

Working at the stall had successfully kept Daphne's mind off the ordeal of her first class at Miss Pettigrew's, but later, as she set off, following the directions Joe had written out for her, her stomach knotted up again. She looked down at her shabby St. Jude's gym tunic. *I'll stand out like a sore thumb in this*, she worried. Well, it couldn't be helped. It was the only thing in her meagre wardrobe she could possibly wear. To cheer herself up, she opened the paper bag she carried and peered in at her beautiful new ballet slippers, a kind gift from Sheila and Harry Cheadle.

The Pettigrew School of Ballet was in an old ware-house, a brisk ten minutes' walk from the market square. Climbing the building's rickety wooden stairs, Daphne heard an out-of-tune piano and a sharp voice calling out commands, "Long, stretched backs, please. Graceful, curved fingers. Don't let your feet roll inwards."

As Daphne came in, the unsmiling woman standing in the middle of the long room clapped her hands and said crisply, "That's all for today, girls and boys."

Oh, no, she looks like an absolute dragon, Daphne thought, her heart pounding.

The class ended with the traditional 'reverence', a curtsy of respect and gratitude for being allowed to dance. Daphne's throat tightened when she saw how the girls were dressed. All of them wore pale pink leotards and tights and had their hair pulled back in neat buns.

She shrank back against a wall. *I haven't got any dance clothes and my hair's all wrong as well*, she thought, feeling terrified and out of place. She stared again at the dancers. They wore shoes laced with satin ribbons.

And they're up on their toes on pointe, Daphne thought,

enviously. She'd read all about that. When you first started dancing you had to wear the sort of ballet slippers she'd been given, made of canvas with an elastic strap over the instep. Pointe shoes, moulded by hand out of several layers of satin, burlap and paste and tied with the ribbons, were longed for by every ballerina in training. But they could only be achieved when your teacher said you were ready for them, when you were strong and skilled enough to go up on your toes for the advanced steps.

Daphne's panic grew as she stared at Miss Pettigrew, who was as thin as a weasel, with a back as straight as a ramrod. *I can do the splits and get my leg straight up over my head. But will that be enough for her?*

The teacher turned and barked, "Daphne Green?"

Daphne straightened her shoulders. "Yes, Miss Pettigrew."

Miss Pettigrew's sharp, disapproving eyes swept over Daphne from head to foot. She took in Daphne's old tunic and white socks, then said, glaring, "Before you come to my next class, please put your hair up tidily."

Speechless, Daphne could only nod.

The room had emptied and, to her puzzlement, was now filling up again with small children. They were dressed as miniature versions of the previous class, except for their ballet slippers, which were just like Daphne's.

"I've put you with the little ones for today, until I see what you can do," Miss Pettigrew said. Miserably embarrassed, Daphne felt her heart plummet.

"I've been informed you've never had a proper ballet lesson and have been teaching yourself from a *book*." The teacher's scornful tones made it very clear exactly what she thought of that.

Without giving Daphne a chance to explain, Miss Pettigrew turned rudely away. She clapped her hands loudly, twice. "Warm-up exercises, girls, please."

Daphne wished she could sink through the floor. Instead she forced herself to take her place at the barre, the long wooden pole attached to the tall mirrors all along one wall.

"No giggling!" Miss Pettigrew snapped. Daphne blushed fiery red. She knew everyone was giggling at her. *And, really,* she thought, *I can't blame them. I look ridiculous towering over them all in my hideous clothes.*

"And ONE, and TWO, and THREE and FOUR, are we eating too much, Edith, dear? Remember, there are no fat ballerinas," Pettigrew snapped. The little girl's eyes filled with tears and she let out a hiccuping sob.

That poor little kid, Daphne sympathised. Pettigrew's cruel. Fear swept through her again.

Miss Pettigrew was coming closer, moving along the line of dancers, adjusting an arm here, a knee there. When she reached Daphne, she let out a squawk of horror. "NO, NO, Daphne! Straighten your leg! Haven't you learned anything *at all* from that book of yours?"

Daphne, struggling to copy the others, was wobbling uncomfortably with one foot flat on the floor and the other up on the barre. *Can't she see I'm trying*, she thought angrily.

But it only got worse as the class went on. Pettigrew had nothing but criticism for her. Even the five basic ballet positions for the feet, which Daphne had so recently taught herself, were wrong apparently. After what seemed to her like eternity, the warm-ups ended.

"Music, please, Fred," Miss Pettigrew called to the ancient man at the piano. "Move to the middle of the room, girls. We shall work on our grand battements and pirouettes."

How to had explained at length why the names in ballet were all in French. It was because ballet had been invented in the 1600s in the Court of King Louis XIV, France's greatest monarch, who'd been nicknamed the Sun King, and who had built the magnificent Palace of

Versailles. The king loved dancing and had a talented teacher called Pierre Beauchamp.Beauchamp had collected an assortment of dance steps from earlier centuries, put them together and made them into 'ballet'. The king took lessons and created a ballet company at court in which he danced himself. He was probably rotten, Daphne had giggled to herself, but all the smarmy courtiers would have had to fall over themselves giving him compliments!

Daphne had memorised all the names of the steps, but, of course, she hadn't had enough time to practise and learn how to do them correctly.

She struggled on as best she could until, at last, the class ended. The young pupils were collected and whisked away. Daphne stayed behind, twisting her hands together with apprehension. *Oh, no,* she thought with dread, as Miss Pettigrew beckoned grimly.

"Look," the teacher said abruptly, "I told Carlo and Maria Green I'd try, but now that I've seen your work, I don't see the point of beating about the bush. You're wasting your time with ballet lessons. I'm afraid you didn't start training early enough. Some of my pupils come to me when they're as young as three." Seeing Daphne's horrified expression, Miss Pettigrew continued a bit less harshly, "I'm sorry but I must tell you that in my opinion, at thirteen it's too late for you. I don't think you can be any kind of a professional dancer, and certainly not a ballerina."

Daphne felt her mind go blank with shock and disappointment. Without a word, she grabbed her things and fled down the stairs and along the empty street. The pain in her heart was so agonising she was afraid she might collapse. She had to stop, doubled up against a brick wall, while she tried to catch her breath.

When she could think clearly again, her first reaction was violent anger. Not at Miss Pettigrew. She was a horrid old bat, but she was only saying what she believed. No, the fury was at herself, for hoping and believing that a mere parcel could hold the key to her past and her future. *Magic, for pity's sake*, she told herself, bitterly. Just because you wanted something desperately didn't mean you were going to get it.

"This is the worst day of my life," Daphne cried out despairingly. She felt huge wrenching sobs shake her whole body, as if she was weeping out all the pain, the loneliness, the hopes and the dreams of her childhood. It went on and on until her head hurt so much it felt as if she had an iron band clamped around it. Wrung out and completely defeated, she bent down, took off her precious ballet slippers, and slowly changed into her street shoes.

As she walked slowly home, she wondered what she could possibly tell the Greens, after all the trouble they'd gone to on her behalf. Would they be so disappointed in her that her fears would come true and they'd send her back to St. Jude's?

But she found she didn't have to say anything at all. Maria heard the front door opening and flew out of the kitchen. When she saw Daphne's anxious, tear-stained face, she opened her arms wide.

"It's all right luv, it's all right," she said softly, hugging Daphne to her. "Me and Carlo and Joe will love you just the same whatever's 'appened."

Daphne gazed gratefully at her, temporarily unable to speak because of the lump of relief in her throat.

With a final, comforting pat Maria let Daphne go. "Tom's come from the Britannia to 'ave supper with us. And Dolly's 'ere, too. You take your time, luv. Just come along to the kitchen when you're ready."

"Oh Maria," Daphne said. "I couldn't face anyone at the moment. Miss Pettigrew said there was no point in me going back there."

Maria's eyes blazed. "Mean old cow!" she said. "Carlo'll see to 'er."

"No, Maria, it was me. Honestly, I was simply dreadful. Would you mind terribly if I didn't come to the kitchen? I couldn't eat any dinner. You can tell everyone why if you like," Daphne said sadly.

"Course I wouldn't mind, luv. You go and I'll bring you in something later."

The first thing Daphne did when she got to her bedroom was to snatch up the book and stockings and shove them as hard as she could right to the back of the top shelf of her wardrobe. "Good riddance!" she said angrily, banging the door shut. "I'm not believing in *you* any more!"

She was lying on her bed, staring at the ceiling, when she heard a soft tap at the door. "You in there, Daphne?" asked Tom. Daphne hesitated. She desperately wanted to be by herself, but she didn't want to be rude after he had so kindly got the tickets for *Swan Lake*.

"It's all right, you can come in," she said. "But don't put on the light please, Tom."

Tom's shadowy figure filled the doorway. "I 'eard," he said. "Maria told us. 'Ard luck, luv. I just came to tell you the Splendide's 'opped it back to Paris. Do you still want to 'ave a look around the Britannia?"

Daphne lay silently, wondering what on earth would be the point of it after this afternoon. But then she remembered Joe and Dolly and Lofty. *They'll still believe in me*, she comforted herself. *I must find out as much as I can about the theatre. I owe it to The Friends. Even though I'll have to face the fact that now I'll never be a ballerina, and dance on the same stage as Ova Andova.*

"'Ow about tomorrow afternoon?" Tom suggested, cheerfully.

"Yes, please, Tom," Daphne replied in a small voice.

Chapter Eight

Dusk was falling as Daphne and Tom reached the Britannia's stage door. Unlocking it with an ornate old key, Tom escorted Daphne inside. She breathed in deeply. "I can smell make-up, and perfume and paint and glue and dust and floor wax and cobwebs and, oh I don't know, oranges or something delicious."

"Well, that's about as good a description of wot all the good theatres smell like backstage as I've ever 'eard," Tom said. "Now, 'ow about a cup of tea before we start? I've got some nice chocolate biscuits."

"I'd love that, Tom."

They had a wonderful time. Tom told Daphne about his life and how he'd become the Britannia's stage door-keeper, then Daphne told Tom about hers and her vow to become a ballerina somehow.

"Orl right, I know you started late," Tom said. "That means you'll just 'ave to be extra clever in finding a way. There's bin many on this stage wot started from nothing and got there by talent and sheer 'ard work."

Daphne smiled at him gratefully, feeling hopeful for the first time since she'd dragged herself home from Miss Pettigrew's. Perhaps becoming a ballerina wasn't a lost cause, after all.

At last Tom looked at his watch. "Good gracious. We'd better get a move on, Daphne. I didn't realise we'd bin talking for so long. Where would you like to start, the stage again? 'Cos you didn't get a chance to see it properly last time."

"Of course, I'd love to go on-stage, but before we do, could you show me all the real behind-the-scenes places?"

"Are you afraid of heights?" Tom asked.

Daphne felt puzzled. "I don't think so, why?" "Come on, then," Tom said mysteriously. He led her behind the stage, right to the back wall of the theatre. A metal ladder fixed to the bricks disappeared upwards, far out of sight.

"Up we go, then. I'll lead the way." Tom climbed nimbly. Daphne followed behind, up and up and up until, looking down, she could see the stage in miniature below, lit by cold, yellow stage work lights.

"This is wot we call the 'fly floor,'" Tom explained.

They stepped off the ladder onto a broad plank walkway than ran the full width of the stage.

"Why's it called the fly floor?" Daphne asked, fascinated. "Do you keep performing flies up here?"

Tom laughed. "You're a sharp one! But it ain't those kind of flies." He pointed. Daphne looked up to where a row of thick ropes were attached to huge, heavy wheels. "Now, look over the safety railing," Tom told her. Leaning over the handrail, Daphne saw the ropes were tautly attached to painted scenery panels dangling high above the stage. "See, when the curtains are closed, the stage 'ands work them winches and 'fly' the scenery on and orf the stage," he explained.

"Oh, I see," Daphne said. "I wondered how it got changed so quickly." Her eyes darted around. "What's this sloping trough for, Tom?"

He picked up one of the big metal balls lying on the floor near it. "'Ere," he said. "Roll that down there."

Daphne did and nearly jumped out of her skin, the roll of thunder was so loud.

"Good, innit?" Tom said, laughing. Just then, they heard someone calling from the stage below, "Tom, is that you up there?"

"Oops!" Tom said. "That's Miss Bailey, the Manager.

I'd better 'otfoot it back down and find out what she wants. Will you be orl right if I leave you 'ere for a few minutes?"

"Of course I will, I'm so lucky to be here, there's tonnes to look at," Daphne said.

"Right, then. Coming Miss B," he called down over the railing. The sound of his footsteps receded back down the ladder.

All by herself in this extraordinary place, Daphne peered around her. Cautiously, she crossed the plank walkway to the other side of the stage. In a dusty corner she saw a pair of mismatched armchairs, their stuffing oozing out. Last week's newspapers lay on the seats. It had to be where the stagehands took their breaks. Behind the chairs was a haphazard pile of tattered cardboard boxes filled with old scripts and scenery diagrams. Daphne bent over for a closer look.

Her heart almost stopped beating.

Sticking out of the nearest box she saw an envelope, yellow with age and sealed with red wax. On the front of it, in elegant, old-fashioned writing, were three words that nearly made her topple over with shock:

'Mademoiselle Daphne Green'.

As Daphne pulled out the envelope with trembling hands, one of the scripts came out with it and fell to the floor. Bending to pick it up, she glanced at the front page, and suddenly her knees gave way. She fell back into the nearest armchair. Because the script was entitled:

The Scarlet Stockings
A Ballet in Two Acts

She laid it beside her in the chair and, frantically, tore open the envelope.

My dear Mademoiselle Green,

*As I imagine you have realised, you have solved the first line of your riddle, '**First, you must find me.**' I offer my sincere congratulations to you, the new owner of the scarlet stockings. It will be up to you to decide their destiny and your own. This you will do by solving the other lines of the riddle. My purpose in this letter is to tell you how the stockings came into existence and to warn you of their unimaginable power.*

After I invented ballet,

Dumbstruck, Daphne stopped reading, her heart racing. Who *wrote* this? Who put it here? Holding her breath, she turned the parchment over to see the signature on the other side. Although it was written in a scrawl adorned with many ornate flourishes, she could read it quite clearly. *Pierre Beauchamp.*

Pierre Beauchamp? The French King's ballet teacher? Who lived in the 1600's. Not possible! Not even *remotely* possible. Daphne shook her head in disbelief.

But, as if pulled by a magnet, slowly her eyes returned to the letter.

After I had invented ballet by combining our own court dances with steps and movements from other centuries, the King and his courtiers performed it at the Royal Court of Versailles. But soon I began to be afraid. What would happen when I died? People forget, they change things and soon, nothing is left. I intended that ballet should live forever, and I searched for a spell to ensure its survival.

I am forbidden to tell you how I came across the spell of the scarlet stockings, but this I must tell you.

The scarlet stockings will not help the lazy. You must do the work required to make you a great dancer. However, they will be your partner, and when you wear them, the spell will help you dance at your very best.

This above all. It is a matter of life and death that

you fully understand that the stockings exist to obey the deepest wishes of your heart. THEREFORE, BEWARE THE CHOICES YOU MAKE!

You are not the first to wear the stockings. Others, such as Auguste Trestis and Maria Taglioni, have come before you. Now they belong to you. Choose well. For in choosing, you yourself will determine whether you live or die. Once you have read the script you will understand.

Farewell.

Daphne looked up from the letter, her face ashen. Auguste Vestris? Marie Taglioni? She'd read about both of them. Auguste Vestris had danced in the 1780s. He was so famous that when he was in London the Houses of Parliament had actually cancelled a session so that its members could attend one of his performances. Taglioni was the first woman to go up on pointe in 1832. *How to Teach Yourself Ballet* had told the almost unbelievable story of how, in 1842, after Taglioni gave her last performance in Russia, a pair of her ballet shoes was bought for a fortune by an admiring fan. He had the shoes cooked and garnished with a special sauce, then he and a group of devoted ballet fans ate them! Did these legendary dancers know what she now knew?

Could she really have been chosen to follow in their footsteps?

With a violent start, Daphne heard Tom's returning footsteps, "Found something to keep you, busy, I see," he greeted her.

Caught off guard, feeling grateful that the light was so dim, Daphne slid the letter carefully between the pages of the script. She must buy time to read them both properly. "Just this old script, Tom. It looks rather interesting. Do you think I could possibly borrow it?" she asked, trying to keep her voice casual.

"Don't see why not, luv. It's bin stuck up 'ere with all the rest of the junk nobody can't be bothered to throw away."

Daphne's look of shining gratitude made him smile. "You'd better get off 'ome," he said. " Maria'll have me guts for garters if you're late for supper! I'll take you onto the stage another time."

They turned towards the ladder. Down by the stage door, Daphne gave Tom a hug, then, clutching the precious script to her, she ran home across the square as if she had wings on her heels.

Chapter Nine

"Good, luv, I'm just dishing up," Maria said when Daphne came rushing into the kitchen. "Did you have a nice time?"

"Wonderful, thank you, Maria. Have I got a minute before supper?"

"If you're quick. Soup ain't no good if it ain't 'ot."

Daphne ran to her room. Standing on tiptoe, she reached into her wardrobe to retrieve the precious objects she'd stuffed away onto the top shelf the night before. Carefully, she put the letter, the script, the book and the stockings under her pillow and drew her coverlet up over them. "There," she said. "I'll have to wait to look at you until everyone's in bed."

"'Ow was that lemon sponge cake, Daphne, luv?" Maria asked at the end of supper. "I'll show you 'ow to make it, tomorrow if you like."

"Mmm, delicious, Maria," Daphne replied. But it

could have been sawdust for all she knew, because she hadn't actually noticed anything she'd eaten.

Go to bed, go to bed, everyone, she wanted to yell in frustration after she'd helped Maria clear the table and wash the dishes. She thought she'd explode if she had to wait a minute longer. She stuck her head round the parlour door to say goodnight to the Greens. In her room, she sat down on the side of the bed, the letter clasped in her hands.

After what seemed like ages, she opened her bedroom door and peeped out. All comings and goings had stopped. The corridor was dark. She got undressed and into her nightgown. At last, she felt it would be safe to begin. Burning with impatience, Daphne opened the script and turned to page one, Act I.

The ballet *The Scarlet Stockings* was about a secret pair of magical stockings which gave their owner unparalleled talent, bringing with it glory, riches and fame. But there was a deadly catch. At the height of their career, the owner, man or woman, had to choose a successor and pass the stockings on. If they broke their promise to do so, death would seek them out.

When Daphne got to this part, she stopped to give her startled mind a chance to catch up with her eyes.

The story was *exactly* the same as Monsieur Beauchamp's warning!

And even more incredible was that the mystery of the scarlet stockings had come into *her* life. Eagerly, she read on.

At the end of Act I, the stockings were in the possession of a beautiful young dancer, as modest as she was talented. In a dramatic solo, the ballerina discovered their power to set her talent aflame. To a thrilling final chord, she leaped through the air and off into the wings in ballet's most spectacular step, the grand jeté. The curtain fell.

Her mind whirling, Daphne put the script down. The ballet was only a story. But the stockings were undeniably a fact. The other girls in the dormitory had all seen them, too. Daphne felt the solid ground of Hoxton slipping away from under her.

Pierre Beauchamp had written she would have to follow the riddle to its end. Now she knew that finding the script was the meaning of the first line. That meant she must now be at line two, *Then, you must follow me*. Follow? Follow where? Hurriedly, she picked up the script and turned to Act II.

Now the ballerina had changed. Her glittering fame

had made her cold and arrogant. Behind the scenes during rehearsal, she stood rigid and unsmiling, occasionally stroking the stockings on her legs, watching as other talented young dancers went through their paces. Her sneering expression and rude behaviour showed her thoughts only too clearly. No one else would *ever* own the scarlet stockings. *She* would go down in history as the greatest ballerina who'd ever lived.

Daphne stopped reading again and sat deep in thought. The ballerina in the story had also been warned of the stockings' power. Then how she could possibly have forgotten that, by choosing to keep them for herself, she was risking her life?

Scene 2 began. Daphne hadn't devoured more than a few paragraphs before she felt an icy chill running through her. The scarlet-clad ballerina had lost her mind, and imagined she was being hunted by a vile demon only she could see. She tried in vain to escape, but she was growing weaker and weaker. The story had begun to merge with her nightmare!

Almost sick with anticipation, Daphne turned to the last page. The abyss of death yawned open. But the magic of the scarlet stockings had deserted the young heroine. She fell in terror to her death, as the curtains closed on a great ominous burst of music.

Slowly, Daphne raised her head. It couldn't all be a coincidence: the riddle, the stockings, Beauchamp's letter, the script and her nightmare. What if the story of the ballet and the facts of her life really were colliding? *Perhaps I CAN become a great ballerina after all, in spite of what Miss Pettigrew said*, she thought with a rush of elation. But, immediately, came fear. The stockings could also cause her death.

Turning the pages, she saw that the script contained much more than just the story of the ballet. There was a full musical score. And there were also many coloured sketches – for costumes, for sets and for props. There was even a complete lighting plan.

On the very last page was a portrait of Pierre Beauchamp himself. Dressed as an elegant French courtier, he wore a dark, curly, shoulder-length wig, striped satin tailcoat, brocade waistcoat, knee britches and high-heeled, buckled shoes. Daphne stared into his intense, dark, painted eyes, until she could have picked the creator of ballet out of a whole palace full of courtiers. Trusting he could hear her, she said, "I give you my solemn word I'll never forget your warning, Monsieur Beauchamp. And I promise to deserve your faith in me. Just as the last line of the riddle commands."

Suddenly she felt she couldn't wait one more minute

to test the stockings. Half excited, half scared, she wondered where she could do it. Her beautiful bedroom was much too small to dance in.

She tiptoed to her door and opened it a crack onto deep, inky silence. Somewhere nearby, a church clock chimed one. Reaching for the scarlet stockings and her ballet slippers, Daphne padded on bare feet to the front door and glided like a shadow down the stairs to the street. The impressive dark bulk of the Britannia stood across the square. It seemed friendly, somehow, as if it was encouraging her. Daphne sat down on her doorstep and put on the stockings. Then, quickly, she slipped into her ballet shoes and stood up, not waiting to see whether the scarlet stockings changed colour or not.

She began to run along the pavement towards the Brittania, her arms stretched wide. Gathering speed, she closed her eyes and whispered, "Please make me a ballerina."

Then she leaped, up towards the silvery half-moon.

She felt weightless, like a snowflake drifting gracefully in the wind. When she opened her eyes, she saw she'd soared so high she could touch the very top of the nearest lamp-post.

PART TWO

'Then, You Must Follow Me'

Chapter Ten

"This just won't DO!" Lofty cried out, anguished. The Friends had gathered in their usual rehearsal space, the well-tended back garden of Dr. and Mrs. Spires' house in Hoxton's leafiest square.

"I haven't seen Daphne's dance number yet, but the rest of us are absolutely rotten!" Lofty continued, desperately. "I forgot my lines. Joe, you haven't learned half your songs." He turned to Dolly. "And what if you can't make that mechanical thingamajig work? If it doesn't, we won't have a Grand Finale."

Joe patted Lofty's shoulder. "Calm down. You know what they always say. It'll be all right on the night. Or, in our case, the day."

"What I always say is we've only got until the weekend until they boo us off the Britannia's steps," Lofty replied. "Save us with your Spanish flamenco, Daphne, I beg you!"

Daphne hugged her secret to her. For the past weeks,

ever since that magical night in the market square, she'd been practising, with the help of the scarlet stockings and her book. She'd searched Hoxton's back streets until she found a smoothly paved dead-end alley, with two or three deserted warehouses stretching along its narrow length. That lane had become her dance studio, and no professional ballerina could have taken their daily classes more seriously or worked harder. Every spare minute she could steal from helping Maria with the housework or Carlo and Joe in the market, she'd used for rehearsal.

"My flamenco will be a lot better when I can dance it in the gorgeous dress Dolly's designed," she said. "I really need the flouncy skirt for some of the move-ments." She picked up her castanets. "Ready, Doll? 'Lady of Spain'?"

Dolly hoisted her instrument over her shoulders and waited until it delivered an accordion's preliminary grunts and wheezes. "Ready!" she announced.

The eyes of Daphne's audience got rounder and rounder as, superbly professional, she clicked her casta-nets, stamped her feet, and swayed to the flamenco's sultry rhythm. When the music came to a halt on her stylish finishing pose, there was complete silence.

Then, Lofty grabbed Daphne in a stupendous hug.

"I knew we desperately needed you in the Friends!" he said.

"Well, you're a dark horse, I must say," Dolly said, grinning. "What an incredible improvement since our first rehearsal. Amazing! Good for you!"

Joe beamed at Daphne with brotherly approval. "Wait till Ma and Pa see *that*. You've done the Greens proud!"

Suddenly it was Friday, the evening of the dress rehearsal. Final costume fittings were underway in the Spires' living room.

"Dolly, you're a blooming *genius!*" Lofty declared, as he pulled the string hidden deep inside the sleeve of his spangled overcoat. Out of nowhere, rows of colourful paper flags popped up on his shoulders. "Is this all from your ma's dressmaking supply?"

"The fabrics are from Mum. I got the flags and the sequins at Heeley's toyshop and everything else I needed at the handyman's store. I'm afraid to say it's all just about cleaned us out, though. Here's your coat, Joe, try it on."

"Never mind, eh, Doll. We'll fill the hat up again tomorrow." Joe replied, confidently.

There was a knock at the door, and Lofty's mother came in with a tray of glasses and a lemonade pitcher. "Goodness!" she said, gazing at Lofty in his red, white, and blue overcoat. "Aren't you smart. Let me see the back!"

Lofty revolved for her inspection. "Our show's called *The Flags of All Nations,* Mother. It's songs and dances and poems and stuff from all over the world. This is our Grand Finale costume. We've all got a coat like this." With a flourish he pulled the string in his sleeve, and, again, the rows of international flags appeared and stood up proudly.

"*Dolly,*" Mrs. Spires said delightedly. "This must be your best ever. I'll tell my husband we've got to get to the Britannia early tomorrow. I hope no one in Hoxton is rash enough to get a burst appendix! Dr. Spires'll be furious if he gets called away from this!"

She sat down next to Daphne. "You're starting at Girls' Independent on Monday, I believe, Daphne. It'll be a bit of a change for you after St. Jude's I should think. Feeling a bit nervous?"

Daphne felt her stomach tighten. "Horribly nervous, Mrs. Spires," she admitted. "I've been trying not to think about it. Honestly, I wish I hadn't got to go at all. I'd much rather get a job so I can earn money for proper ballet lessons. I've got miles to go to catch up with everyone else my age. They all started when they were tiny. I'll be fourteen next week. Lots of people younger than me leave school early and go to work if they come from big families and the parents need the wages to help support everyone."

"And would your new parents approve of that in your case, Daphne?" Lofty's mother asked, gently.

"No, they flipping well wouldn't, Mrs. Spires," Joe cut in. "Dad says we've got to get all the education we can and stay at school until leaving age, fifteen. He's pleased as a dog with three tails that our schools have taught us to speak 'proper.' He says Green's can get along without either of us going into the business. We're supposed to cover the name Green with academic glory!"

"I do rather agree with him, I'm afraid, Daphne, dear. Lofty's told me how much you want to be a professional ballerina. We must try hard to think of something." Mrs. Spires patted Daphne's arm sympathetically as she got up to go. "Well, I must get on. Good luck for tomorrow, everyone."

While Dolly fussed over the sleeves of Joe's costume, Daphne sat down on the sofa and opened the latest copy of the newspaper called *The Stage*. Lofty bought one every week. "It's got casting notices for every show in England," he'd explained to Daphne. "And all the news and gossip you've got to keep up with if you're serious about a career in the theatre. All I can do for now, though, is read about it, worse luck. Because I promised Dad that, before I went on any auditions, I'd try to get into the same university he went to in Cambridge, and get what he calls 'a proper degree.'"

All of a sudden, Daphne stopped turning the pages, her attention riveted by a bordered half-page advertisement:

OPPORTUNITY AS PERSONAL ASSISTANT TO MAGDA MAGELLAN
Candidates may apply between the hours of 11a.m to 2 p.m.
No. 60 Park Lane.
Ask for Mrs. Crunge.

Magda Magellan! England's most beautiful, most famous musical comedy star! All over the world, from Cairo to Copenhagen, her throaty, inimitable voice could be heard husking out 'Alone in Paradise With You', the song that was whistled by bicycling errand boys and hummed by polo- playing dukes, the song that had launched her glittering career.

Turning her back to make sure no one was watching her, Daphne quickly copied out the advertisement and stuffed it into her pocket.

"Ready for you now, Daphne," Dolly called. "Here's your coat. And I've got your flamenco costume for you to try on, too." As Daphne got up, Dolly said, "And you other two can stop nattering. You're interfering with my work. Buzz off and do something useful! Rehearse!"

"Terrifying, isn't she!" Joe said.

Lofty pretended to cower. "Let us depart from hence, friend, lest we feel the lash of her furious ire!" They departed, snickering.

A week later, Carlo sat at the kitchen table, reading the *Hoxton Gazette* while he had breakfast. Suddenly, he gave such a huge yell that Maria nearly dropped the frying pan. "Cor, luv, come and look at this!" he shouted. "Bloody marvellous, excuse my language!"

The photograph took up almost the whole of the newspaper's front page. It showed the Friends waving to the applause, Dolly's flags gaily in place on the shoulders of their costumes. The caption read:

Talented Hoxton youngsters perform in front of the Britannia.

Hundreds in the crowd cheered the brilliant flamenco dancing of Miss Daphne Green.

The kitchen door flew open and Daphne rushed in. "Has the post come yet?" she asked urgently.

"No, it 'asn't, but *this* 'as," Carlo said, beaming. "Look wot they've written about your dancing. That'll show that old fool Pettigrew wot she's missed!"

"Oh, my GOODNESS!" Daphne shrieked. The hard work she'd done with the help of the scarlet stockings had resulted in her first rave review! "JOE!" she yelled down the hallway. "Get in here!"

Carlo thumped her on the back in congratulation. "A free cauliflower today for anyone wot mentions this article," he shouted.

"Morning, all," the postman said, walking into the kitchen. No one in Hoxton ever bothered to lock their front door. "Got a quick cuppa for me, Maria?" he asked. While Maria was pouring it out, the postman took some letters out of the bag over his shoulder and handed one to Daphne.

"Something for you, today, luv," he said with a wide smile.

Chapter Eleven

The smart cream and yellow General Omnibus shuddered to a stop. The voice of the conductor bawled out, "Hyde Park Corner, ladies and gents, Hyde Park Corner. Next stop, Park Lane."

Daphne gazed out of the window at the busiest quarter of a mile in central London. The chaos was almost overwhelming, with automobiles breaking down, horses rearing, traffic going off in every direction, and people continuously honking or yelling for right of way.

For relief, she looked out, past the traffic, to the colourful flowerbeds, arching trees and peaceful green open spaces of Hyde Park. Immaculately turned-out riders exercised their horses on Rotten Row, the sawdust ring circling the perimeter of the park. The polished harnesses glinted in the morning sun.

Daphne glanced down with pleasure at her favourite of the new dresses Dolly had made for her. This one, pleated in the softest pale blue cotton, had ribbon trim at the waist and sleeves. Daphne opened her matching handbag and drew out the letter the postman had brought her. She'd grabbed it from him that day, before anyone in the kitchen could express surprise at the luxurious quality of the envelope. "Just a note from Sister Mary E," she'd rushed to say in reply to Maria's questioning glance. Telling a lie had felt awful. When she was a little girl, Daphne had given a promise to Sister Mary Euphoria always to be truthful.

But that was before the scarlet stockings had entered her life. Everything was different now. She'd do what she must to follow the riddle's trail.

Earlier today, Daphne had lied to Maria again, when she'd said she was meeting a friend from her new school to discuss homework. "Back for tea," she'd called from her bedroom, before racing out of the front door and down the stairs to avoid questions about why she was so dressed up.

"Park Lane, ladies and gents, Park Lane," the conductor called out cheerily. Nervously, Daphne smoothed the skirt of her dress and pulled on her lacy white cotton gloves. She'd put her hair up, in the hope it would make her look old enough to be someone's personal assistant. She felt the omnibus judder to a stop.

"Do you know where number sixty Park Lane is, please?" she asked the bus conductor.

He pointed to a row of impressive mansions with graceful windows overlooking Hyde Park. "Mind 'ow you go," he said, hopping off the bus and gallantly offering his arm to Daphne as she stepped down. "Nice to see such a pretty gel in the morning. Does your 'eart good." With a last appreciative look, he got back on, cheerfully whistling off-key. The omnibus lumbered away.

"Let's see, number fifty-seven, fifty-eight, fifty-nine and *there* it is!" Daphne said with relief. Number sixty was too beautiful to be true. She climbed the marble steps, and paused for a moment to breathe in the scent of the yellow roses growing in stone pots on either side of the dark green front door. Then, to give herself courage, she said aloud solemnly, like an incantation, "I have been chosen by destiny."

Lifting the heavy, bronze door knocker in the shape of a globe of the world, Daphne rapped smartly, twice. She waited. And waited. At last she heard the sound of footsteps shuffling towards her. The door swung silently open to reveal the tallest, boniest person Daphne had ever seen. He was dressed in rusty black, and his domed head was fringed with a ring of wispy hair dyed a deep, unconvincing auburn.

Towering above Daphne, he croaked out "Yessssssss?"

Daphne tried to speak, but her mouth was so dry she couldn't get the words out.

"Speak up, young lady. I'm a bit hard of hearing."

"Who is it, Crunge?" a neat, grey-haired woman in a blue dress and a white apron called out as she whisked through the entrance hall holding a feather duster.

"Just a minute," snapped Crunge. "I'm finding out."

Rolling her eyes good-naturedly, the woman disappeared through a door at the side of the hall.

Clearing her throat, Daphne spoke up loudly and clearly. "I'm Daphne Green. I have an interview with Miss Magellan."

"Miss Magellan is not at home," Crunge boomed. "But you may see my wife, Mrs. Crunge. Please enter and I shall conduct you to the kitchen." He moved off at a creaking pace. Daphne followed him, marvelling at the glamour of the glimmering chandeliers, the floor-to-ceiling portraits of the exquisite Miss Magellan, the black-and-white chequerboard marble floor, the gilded rails of the sweeping staircase, and the graceful arrangements of flowers everywhere filling the air with fragrance.

Daphne felt as if she'd stepped into a dream of

unimaginable glamour. *I belong here,* she thought, her whole body stiffening with her passionate determination to make this dream her daily reality.

Crunge pushed open a door covered in a dark green material, which turned out to lead 'backstage'. Following him down the passageway, Daphne was dimly aware of lots of shadowy rooms leading off from it, where sinks and storage cupboards lurked.

"In here," Crunge boomed, opening the door to a kitchen which looked to Daphne to be at least ten times bigger than the one at home. Shining copper pots and pans hung from the walls. There was a vast oven. A huge pine table, surrounded by cushioned cane chairs, took up the middle of the floor. Sunlight beamed in from the windows, where tubs of cheerful red geraniums stood on the deep ledges.

"Well then, Crunge," came the pleasant voice of the woman Daphne had seen in the hall. "Found out what the young lady wants, have you?"

Crunge cleared his throat and said pompously, "The young person has come to apply for a job with us. Her name is Daphne Green."

"I'm just putting the kettle on, dear. Crunge and me usually have a nice cup of tea at this time of the morning. Will you join us?"

"Yes, please," Daphne replied gratefully. 'If it isn't too much trouble."

Mrs. Crunge shook her head, smiling, as she lit the gas flame under the tin kettle. "Now then, let's introduce ourselves properly. I'm Mrs. Crunge, Miss Magellan's housekeeper and cook. And you've met Mr. Crunge, he's the butler and chauffeur here."

"You haven't chosen anyone for the job yet, have you?" Daphne blurted out.

The Crunges exchanged a strange look, one that Daphne couldn't interpret at all. Then Mrs. Crunge said, "No, we haven't found anyone to suit so far. Miss Magellan is *most* particular."

Daphne breathed a silent thank-you. "I know it's a very big opportunity. Do you think I might have a chance?"

"Depends," Mrs. Crunge said mysteriously. "We won't know till Madam looks you over." The kettle whistled and Mrs. Crunge occupied herself with a big brown teapot. "The cups and plates if you please, Mr. Crunge. You'll join us in a slice of sponge cake, luv, won't you?" Mrs. Crunge asked Daphne. "I baked it fresh this morning."

Daphne, twisting her hands nervously, replied, "Yes please, Mrs. Crunge. But when will I be able to meet Miss Magellan?"

"You've just missed her. Madam's gone off to the theatre for her Saturday matinée performance. She may come home before the evening show or she may not. She'll telephone if she wants Crunge to come and pick her up."

"What time will the matinée be over?" Daphne asked anxiously, mentally reviewing the return omnibus time-table.

"If she does come home to rest between shows, it'll be about five," Mrs. Crunge said, handing Daphne a plate with a generous slice of cake on it.

"I'll wait," Daphne said firmly, sipping at the tea and thinking she could pass the time and make a good impression by asking Mrs. Crunge if she needed any help in the kitchen. When she'd finished her cake, she spoke up.

"I won't say no," the cook replied. "Madam's always hungry when she gets home on matinée days. Let's see, perhaps a nice salmon soufflé and some chilled asparagus, seeing as how it's a hot day. And a sherry trifle for afters. You can take the bones out of the fish, if you'd be so kind, dear." She handed Daphne a brown cotton apron. "Have you ever done any cooking?"

"Yes, we were taught a few things at St. Jude's, the orphanage where I grew up, and since I was adopted,

I've been learning how to bake. We're inviting some girls from St. Jude's and one of the Sisters for tea tomorrow."

"An orphan, are you?" Crunge asked.

What a gloomy question, Daphne thought. *He seems like a gloomy sort of person generally.*

"Tell us about yourself, luv," Mrs. Crunge said encouragingly.

So, while she cleaned and boned the fish, Daphne described the Greens and Hoxton and the performances of The Best of Friends. "I've brought our newspaper clipping to show to Miss Magellan, if you think she might be interested."

"Well, I never," Mrs. Crunge said. "I should think Madam would be interested. She grew up in the East End like you. She was discovered performing in a local talent show in the Shoreditch Church Hall when she was about your age."

"No! Shoreditch is only a mile or two from Hoxton. Who discovered her?"

"Ever heard of George Cardew, the theatrical agent?" Mrs. Crunge asked.

"I haven't, but my friend Lofty Spires probably has. He's going to be an actor."

"Well, this George Cardew's a good chap. He'd come

to the talent show because it was his cousin who was putting it on. Madam was tap dancing and singing Pack Up Your Troubles in Your Old Kit Bag, and Smile, Smile, Smile."

"Carlo sings that. It's a soldier's song from the War," Daphne said, excited. "So, then what happened?"

"He sniffed out talent, didn't he? It wound up with him paying for Miss Magellan — only she wasn't Magda Magellan then, she was Maggie Morris — to come to London with her mum, and to go to the Royal Academy of Dramatic Art for lessons."

Daphne drank all of this in. "How long did she go for?"

"I believe it was three years. She told me she had to do acting, and dancing, and movement, and what she called voice lessons."

"Mr. Cardew must have known he'd get all his money back later."

"Yes, luv, he did and he was right. You should see his offices now. A bit different from what they used to be when Madam first saw them. As soon as she finished at the Academy Mr. Cardew got her an audition for a small part in a musical. He had to do some fast-talking to get her seen, Madam said. But he did it, and they liked her so much they gave her a song in the show."

"*Alone in Paradise with You*," Daphne interrupted eagerly. "Yes, I know, I've read about that." She put down the boning knife. "I think I've finished the fish."

Mrs. Crunge came over and examined Daphne's work closely. "Very nice, dear. If you'll wash your hands you can whip up the cream for the trifle next."

From the sink, Daphne asked, "Does Miss Magellan's mother live here, too?"

"Bless you, no. She's got a cottage by the sea now. Said she was getting on and couldn't keep up with Madam and all her shows and her travelling and her parties. Of course, Madam bought her the cottage. Down south in Cornwall it is, in a little fishing village called St. Mawes."

Daphne was thrilled to be finding out so much interesting information. She looked forward to enthralling Joe and Dolly and Lofty with it all when she got home. WHEN SHE GOT HOME! Panicking, she realised she didn't have a clue when that would be. It was past teatime already. *Maria'll be worried stiff. When on earth am I going to meet Miss Magellan?*

"I don't think she'll be coming now, luv," Mrs. Crunge said sympathetically, seeing Daphne's anxious face. "She'll be getting ready for the eight o'clock."

Oh, no, Daphne thought. But then she had an idea.

Hesitantly she asked, "Could I possibly borrow Miss Magellan's telephone?" Crunge frowned. "I've used one before, our friends have got one. I'll be extremely careful, I promise. I'll repay Miss Magellan for the call, of course."

"Well, I suppose under the circumstances," Crunge said grudgingly. "You may give the tuppence to me and I'll make sure Madam receives it."

But the operator had bad news. "I'm terribly sorry, Miss," she said. "I can't get Mr. and Mrs. Cheadle, there's a fault on the line, I'm afraid. But, don't worry, Repairs have told me they'll have it sorted out by tomorrow, around lunchtime."

This information sent Daphne into a complete panic. *It'll have to be a telegram, then*, she told herself. *I hope it doesn't scare them to death when it's delivered.*

She asked for a piece of paper and scribbled:

```
Had to go to the West End. Sorry,
delayed. Will explain when I get home
        later tonight. Sorry. Daphne.
```

The long face of Mr. Crunge peered over her shoulder. "What are you doing, girl?" he asked. "Telegram is it? Give it to me, I'll take it to the telegraph office for you.

They're closed now but I don't suppose it's URGENT, is it?" He cackled loudly at his own wit.

"No need for one of your silly jokes," Mrs. Crunge said disapprovingly. "You can see the girl's proper worried. I'm ever so sorry, luv, the telegraph office closes at five."

Daphne's heart sank. She started to gather up her handbag and gloves. *This is a disaster*, she thought. *I'll simply have to go*. Then the telephone bell jangled outside in the passageway. Crunge shuffled off to answer it. Daphne could hear his loud voice booming, "Yes, Madam. Certainly, Madam." He creaked back into the kitchen. "That was Madam," he said, unnecessarily, because Daphne and Mrs. Crunge had both heard his end of the conversation quite clearly. "Said she's tired," he went on. "She wishes me to bring her home imme-diately after the curtain. Says she'll take her make-up off here tonight."

"I can't say I'm surprised," Mrs. Crunge told Daphne. "She's been out till all hours every night this week. Dancing and such. Even she gets worn out sometimes. Do her good to be here on her own without all her friends with her, for a change."

Slowly, Daphne put down her things. *Straight after the show*, she thought. *And by herself.* There never would be a better opportunity to convince Miss Magellan of exactly how much she needed Daphne as her personal assistant. Whatever the dire consequences might be, she had no choice now but to stay.

Embarrassed, she realised she could hardly keep her eyes open. Yawning, she asked shyly, "Mrs. Crunge, is there anywhere I could possibly sit quietly until later?"

Looking sympathetically at Daphne's flushed, nervous face, Mrs. Crunge said, "Crunge, why don't you take Daphne to the conservatory. It's always nice and cool. You can wait there, luv, with pleasure."

Gratefully, Daphne followed the butler's tall, bent back out into the main part of the house. Off a short passageway on the ground floor was an airy room filled with flowering plants and ferns. The walls and ceiling were made of glass, looking out over the mansion's pretty garden. With the soft evening light coming in through the open windows, the room was made even more pleasant by the sound of water trickling from a fountain on a wall nearby. With a sigh of relief, Daphne sank down into a deep cushioned armchair and put her legs up on its footstool. She didn't even hear Crunge go because she fell asleep immediately.

The sound of voices woke her.

"Tired out, poor thing. She's been waiting since

eleven o'clock this morning," Mrs. Crunge said. Daphne jerked upright in her chair. The room was dark but she could see a slender figure standing next to the house-keeper in the backlit doorway.

"I hope she doesn't get tired often," a husky voice answered.

Daphne rose gracefully to her feet. "Good evening, Miss Magellan," she said. "Please forgive my falling asleep. I've been rather nervous waiting to meet you."

Magda laughed lightly. "You're not the first person to be nervous about meeting me. I suppose I *am* rather frightful! Shall we go up to the drawing room? We can talk while I eat my supper." She glided off, her turquoise satin dressing gown sweeping along the floor behind her.

Then, you must follow me, Daphne thought, her heart pounding as she nervously followed in the star's glamorous wake.

Chapter Twelve

The drawing room, lit softly by silk-shaded lamps, was one flight up. Daphne watched Magda settle herself in a comfy, cream-coloured armchair, her supper tray with the salmon soufflé on her lap. She saw the actress had taken off her stage make-up, revealing the glowing, flawless skin beneath. A half-empty champagne glass stood on a small table at her elbow. The diamonds on her slim fingers flashed as she motioned Daphne to sit opposite her.

Whatever time can it be, Daphne thought anxiously. *I'm sure I've missed the last bus. Concentrate!* she told herself fiercely, staring at Magda's perfectly shaped mouth, beautifully modelled cheekbones, long blonde hair and the famous, startlingly green eyes.

Daphne marvelled at how graceful, how effortless Magda's movements were. It was just like watching Madame Andova walk down that staircase. *It must be what people mean when they talk about star quality*, she thought longingly. *I'd give anything to learn it.*

"Do tell me about yourself," Magda's unforgettable voice said.

Daphne hesitated because it was so tricky. Say too much and she might bore Magda. Say too little and she might not get the job.

Crossing her fingers, Daphne explained how she'd always known she was born to dance. How she'd made up steps from the time she could walk, and devoured everything about dancing from every book and newspaper she'd ever read. And how she'd managed to convince the Reverend Mother to let her practise every day except Sunday, even though the Reverend Mother had said, "absolutely not" at first.

"I see," Magda said. "Very inventive of you. And were you ever able to dance for an audience?"

"Well, for the other girls, of course, and at our Christmas concerts for the governors I did, and then, after I was adopted —" she paused and dug in her handbag. "My new brother's part of a group of street entertainers and they invited me to join them. Would you like to see our press clipping?"

Magda read it with interest. "I see your dancing got a rave review. Well done!"

With a silent prayer of thanks to the scarlet stockings, Daphne said, "I had a lot of help with that flamenco number." She rushed on, "I'm going to be a ballerina."

Magda looked at her thoughtfully. "Hmm, lots of stamina required for that. And how are you intending to pursue your ballet career?"

"If I'm lucky enough to get the job as your personal assistant, I'd save my salary and take ballet lessons in the evenings."

Magda sat thinking, while Daphne waited impatiently. Then, the star's lovely emerald eyes looked straight into Daphne's dark, hopeful ones. "Yes," she said, slowly. "I think you will suit."

Next morning, in Hoxton, Constable Bodger dropped his badger-hair shaving brush back into its bowl of soapy water as the telephone shrilled. Buttoning his uniform jacket, in case it was official business, the sturdy constable went into the next room and picked up the receiver. "'Oxton police station," he announced. His face cleared when he heard Daphne's voice at the other end of the line. He listened to her rapid explanation of how she'd missed the last omnibus, then said in a lecturing kind of way, "You're going to 'ave some explaining to do, young lady. Carlo and Maria 'ave already bin round this morning. They're 'arf mad with worry. I should think they didn't sleep a wink." He listened again. "Orl right then, don't carry on. I'll go round there straight away and say you'll be back soon. And mind you are," he added in his 'official warning to offenders' voice.

Subdued, Daphne put down the telephone and went back into the kitchen where the Crunges were having their breakfast. There was a boiled egg and some toast waiting for her, but she didn't feel like eating it now. The excitement she'd felt when she'd woken in the attic bedroom, wrapped in one of Mrs. Crunge's ample nightgowns, had all drained away. She felt sick with anxiety and dread.

The hands of the kitchen clock tocked round to eight o'clock. "I must go, they're terribly worried about me at home."

Mrs. Crunge clicked her tongue, sympathetically. "Off you go then, luv. When could you start with us?"

"Would a week from today be all right, do you think? That would give me time to say a proper goodbye to my family and friends in Hoxton."

"I expect we'll manage until then. I'll let Madam know."

"And when you come back, mind you use the staff door," Crunge said pompously, pointing to the one in the corner of the kitchen.

Riding home in the rattling omnibus, Daphne felt her spirits begin to rise again. *Wait till I tell them I'm Magda Magellan's new personal assistant! Even Carlo will have to agree that's worth leaving school for*, she told herself gleefully.

As she put her key in the lock and opened the front door, she could hear the sound of subdued conversation coming from the parlour. They were all waiting for her ... Carlo, Maria, Joe, Lofty, Dolly, Tom, and Sheila and Harry Cheadle. Flinching, Daphne saw that Maria's eyes were red and puffy and Carlo's clothes were rumpled, as if he'd slept in them.

"Where 'ave you bin?" Carlo roared, furiously. "We was worried sick until Constable Bodger came round 'ere this morning."

"Couldn't you 'ave let us know? Maria demanded in an angry voice Daphne had never heard her use before.

Daphne had intended to apologise, she really had. The last thing she'd intended was to cause such horrible worry.

But, looking around at all the disapproving faces, she pretended not to care. *This is my chance to be somebody*, she told herself. *Nobody's going to make me feel guilty about that!* "Well, you won't have to worry about me any more because I won't be here," she said sharply. "I'll be very busy in Park Lane being Magda Magellan's personal assistant!"

"You can't be talking about *the* Magda Magellan?" Joe asked.

"Yes, I am," Daphne replied triumphantly. There was a stunned silence.

"You'd better tell us wot you've bin doing," Maria said.

So, Daphne explained about seeing the advertisement at Lofty's, and writing to Miss Magellan for an interview, and working out the right omnibus route to Park Lane, and using her saved-up pocket money for the fare. As she spoke, Daphne saw Joe cautiously shooting her a look of admiration, and she felt a rush of confidence.

"I did try to contact Mr. and Mrs. Cheadle, but their phone machine was out of order, then I tried to send a telegram, but the office was closed." Still nobody said anything, so she went on explaining, up to the moment she'd been told she'd suit. "But by then it was so late, I had to sleep at Miss Magellan's."

"This is orl a load of rubbish," Carlo said, glaring. "Wot does a so-called personal assistant do, then?"

"Oh, answer the telephone and write letters, and bring things Miss Magellan's forgotten to rehearsal, and attend her opening nights," Daphne said, improvising.

Actually, she didn't know exactly what she'd be doing. She just knew it would be exciting. "Miss Magellan said there'd be a little light housework thrown in, but I don't mind because I'll be earning money for ballet lessons with a proper teacher." She stumbled to a halt at the sight of Carlo's stern face.

"You can get a letter orf in the post straightaway. You'll 'ave to explain to Miss Magellan that your parents 'ave refused to let you leave school to go to work for 'er."

Daphne jumped up, stretching out a pleading hand. "Carlo, *please*."

"I've said no, gel. And that's my last word on the subject until after you've finished at Girls' Independent. If you still want 'er job then, and there's a job for you to 'ave, we'll think about it. So that's that. I'm orf to open the stall." The front door slammed behind him.

And Daphne felt her sparkling, magical future break into a million jagged pieces and come smashing down around her.

Chapter Thirteen

Tom looked steadily into Daphne's blazing eyes. "If I have to wait until I leave school to get a job and start proper ballet lessons, I'll never, ever be a ballerina," Daphne said passionately. "It was you who gave me the idea. You said I'd have to be extra clever to find a way. So, I thought of one. Seeing that advertisement was fantastically lucky. *You* know what a job with Magda Magellan might lead to. You said lots of performers start from nowhere, just like me, and get to the top by sheer hard work. So will I. I'll work till I drop to catch up with the other dancers, even if it means staying up all night, every night. Miss Magellan's got an actual ballroom in her house. She said I could use it in my spare time to practise in."

"But what about yer education, luv?" Tom asked worriedly. "Carlo's got 'is heart set on you going to school until leaving age. I know 'im when 'ee's set on something. 'Ee was the same when 'ee was a kid. Stubborn."

"I know, and that's why you're the only person I can

think of who could get him and Maria to change their minds," Daphne said desperately.

But Tom shook his head. "Sorry, luv, it's not up to me to tell Carlo wot to do. 'Ee's your Dad, now."

"I thought you might say that, but listen to my idea. If, after a year at Miss Magellan's, I haven't found a first-class ballet teacher who says I can be good enough to dance professionally, I'll come back to Hoxton and finish my education. I'm just asking Carlo to give me one year, that's all, Tom."

Tom took off his spectacles and rubbed his eyes. "That seems fair enough."

"I'll put it in writing, like a proper business arrangement, if Carlo wants me to," Daphne said urgently.

Slowly, Tom put his glasses back on. "Orl right, I can see you've given this a lot of thought, so I'll give it a try," he said. "But don't get yer 'opes up too much."

"Tom, you angel, I'll never forget you for this. Could you be even more angelic and come back now with me from the Britannia to talk to Carlo and Maria?"

Tom stood up. "No time like the present, eh?"

Daphne paced up and down the hallway outside the kitchen. The door was closed, but even so, she could hear Tom trying to explain something and Carlo shouting.

The kitchen door suddenly banged open. "I told 'er NO. And no it still is." Carlo stood there, looking upset and angry. When he saw Daphne, he shook his head and said in a quieter voice, "I'm responsible for you now, young lady. And you'll just 'ave to trust that I know wot's best."

"But, Carlo…"

"No buts. That letter to Miss Magellan is going orf in the post first thing tomorrow."

Tom appeared behind Carlo's shoulder. Daphne sent him a pleading look. But she saw his mouth move in the silent words, "Sorry, luv, I tried." With a sob, she ran into her bedroom, closing the door hard behind her.

An unhappy silence hung the kitchen. "I'd better be going," Tom said. He gave it one last try. "She's a good gel, Carlo. She just wants a chance."

"I feel sorry for 'er, but that don't mean I'm going to change my mind," Carlo said. "For 'er own good, she's got to finish at Girls' Independent, like I told 'er."

Joe walked Tom to the front door. "I had a horrible feeling Dad wasn't going to agree. This is going to break the poor girl's heart," he said, sadly.

Daphne sat on her bed, *How to Teach Yourself Ballet* open on her knees. She'd been so sure she was on the right track about *Then, you must follow me*. At last, weary and confused, she put the book down. *I suppose they're not deliberately trying to wreck my life,* she thought despairingly. *It's only because they've got such high hopes for me that they want me to stay at school. But they're wrong, why can't they see that?*

She might never get another chance to work for Miss Magellan. *It's so unfair!* she fumed, as she undressed. *Carlo didn't even let Tom explain my idea.*

Although she'd quickly fallen into a dull, heavy sleep, Daphne woke up with a start. Her bedside clock read two o'clock. The memory of Carlo's angry voice came flooding back. Her stomach churned. It was no good. She couldn't go back to sleep. She'd have to get up and make herself some cocoa.

Cup in hand, she crept into the parlour and sank unhappily down into the welcoming, velvety depths of the Plonkit. Then she heard footsteps in the hallway. Maria appeared in the doorway in her comfy old dressing gown and woolly slippers, her thick, shiny plait of hair hanging over her shoulder. "I thought, I 'eard you," she said, sitting down on the Plonkit, and putting her arm around Daphne's hunched shoulders.

At Maria's affectionate touch, Daphne felt the resentment and hurt inside her thawing. She did love Carlo and Maria. They were doing what they thought was right. But they didn't know what she knew. They didn't know about the scarlet stockings and she couldn't tell them. The riddle said, *Then, you must follow me*. So she had. And *she* had got the job from among all the other people who must have applied. That proved it was meant to be.

Gathering all her courage, she burst out, "Oh, Maria, I'm so very sorry for making you all worry. But Carlo didn't even let Tom explain my idea."

"Wot idea, luv?"

"About letting me go to Miss Magellan's. Only for a year. Then, if getting ballet lessons doesn't work, or if I'm not any good, I'll give up my dream of being a ballerina. I'll come home and work really hard at school until I finish. I solemnly promise."

Maria stared searchingly into Daphne's face. Then, after what seemed like an eternity, she said slowly, "Wot Carlo and me've got to think about is this. We'd never forgive ourselves if we stood in the way of yer dreams. And that's wot we would be doing if we don't let you go to Miss Magellan's and try yer best." She hugged Daphne closely to her.

"We'd miss you something 'orrible, luv. But leave it to me. I'll talk to yer Dad in the morning."

★ ★ ★

Lofty raised his glass of cider. "The Best of Friends won't be the same without you," he said, "but I gladly propose a toast to the new personal assistant to the one and only Magda Magellan."

"To Daphne Green and Magda Magellan," Joe and Dolly chorused. The afternoon sun shone down on the four of them, sitting on the grass in Lofty's back garden.

"You're the envy of every single girl at Independent, you know," Dolly said with a grin.

"But, Carlo and Maria going to talk to the Headmistress was supposed to be a secret," Daphne protested.

"Fat chance. The whole school's laying bets on whether you'll be back in a year or not!"

"See, you're already famous," Lofty said admiringly, waving his glass in the air.

"I'll make up for leaving the Friends in the lurch as soon as I can," Daphne said apologetically. "I'm supposed to get a week's holiday a year. I can join you again then if you still want me."

"Just promise you'll remember us when you're a star," Joe said. "Me more than the other two, of course, because I'm your brother!"

With snorts of disgust, Lofty and Dolly pelted him with scones from the tea tray.

Very early the next day, a send-off committee,

composed of the Friends, the Greens, the Cheadles and Tom, waited with Daphne by the market's omnibus stop. As the vehicle lumbered into sight, Carlo put a paper bag of apples into Daphne's hand. "A little reminder of Greens' Fruit and Veg, luv, so you don't forget us."

Gratefully, Daphne put the apples down by the small suitcase she'd borrowed from the Cheadles and turned to hug Carlo and Maria. There were two words she'd desperately wanted to say to them for weeks now, but she hadn't been able to get them out.

"As if I ever could, Mum, Dad," she whispered.

Then, even Dolly had to get out her handkerchief.

The kitchen door at Park Lane was at the bottom of some steps at the side of the house. Through its glass panel, Daphne could see Mrs. Crunge stirring something on the stove. Crunge, in his shirtsleeves, sat reading the morning paper at the kitchen table. At Daphne's firm knock, he got up to let her in.

"I'm here," Daphne announced cheerfully.

Crunge's gloomy face looked even gloomier than before. "No!" he said, sarcastically. "Are you really? I thought you were a ghost."

Daphne was crushed until Mrs. Crunge said, "You

don't want to take any notice of him, dear. It's just another of his silly jokes. You'll soon get used to them, then you'll ignore them like I do!"

"Well, thank you very much," Crunge said, returning to the table and huffily slurping his cup of tea. "If you ask me, there's far too many women underfoot in this house. A man can't even read the newspaper in peace."

"Come on, Daphne," Mrs. Crunge said briskly. "Madam will be ringing for her breakfast tray soon. You'd better bring that suitcase upstairs and get changed."

"Changed?" Daphne said, puzzled, looking down at her smart blouse and skirt. They were among the nicest things Dolly had made for her. "Won't what I'm wearing do?"

Mrs. Crunge gave Daphne a piercing look. "Come along," she said. Panting from the climb up three flights of stairs to the attic, the housekeeper opened the door of the room where Daphne had spent the night. Laid out neatly on the bed were a black dress, white apron and cap, black stockings and black shoes that buttoned across the instep.

Daphne's mouth fell open. "But," she said stuttering, 'that's a m-m- maid's uniform."

Chapter Fourteen

"I thought I was supposed to be Miss Magellan's personal assistant," Daphne said in shock.

"You'll find out Madam likes to get value for money. Comes of growing up so poor in Shoreditch. She's never got over it. So you'll be doing the housework, too. You're going to be a very busy girl with all of that, as well as helping Madam with her hair and clothes and telephoning and such. Hurry up, now." The door closed on the housekeeper's plump back.

Moving like a sleepwalker, Daphne opened the suitcase. As if mocking her, the scarlet stockings lay where she'd packed them, right on the top. A maid! *Surely, Then, you must follow me doesn't mean I'm supposed to be a maid*, she told herself. She slammed the suitcase shut again. *I'll die before I wear a uniform and do housework*, she vowed. *I'd rather go back to school.*

But, how could she creep back to Hoxton and have everyone either laughing at her or pitying her? She sank slowly down on the bed, trying to work it out in her head. *The scarlet stockings won't do my work for me*, she reasoned. *Monsieur Beauchamp said they'd help me, but it's up to me in the end. I must have serious ballet lessons, and I must practise till I drop. Which means I must take this job.*

Sighing, she got undressed and put on the uniform. After a quick, disgusted look into the cracked mirror above her battered chest of drawers, she banged the bedroom door behind her and ran downstairs to the kitchen.

"There you are, just in time. Madam's rung her bell for her breakfast." Mrs. Crunge pointed to a row of bell panels on the wall. The one marked Bedroom #1 was lit up. Expertly removing hot toast from under the grill, the cook wrapped it in a linen napkin. Then she handed Daphne a tray with slices of exotic fruit on a pretty flowered plate, with matching china and a little teapot. A single deep yellow rose bloomed in a cut-glass vase. "Go up the stairs to the first-floor landing," Mrs. Crunge instructed. "Madam's room is the first on the left, behind the double doors."

Daphne's feet didn't make a sound on the thickly-carpeted stairs. She knocked softly and heard a husky voice say, "Come in." A bump under the covers sat itself upright as Daphne drew back the curtains, trying not to stare at Magda's blush pink silk nightgown with the matching chiffon rose on one shoulder. She must remember every beautiful detail for Dolly.

"Oh, it's you. Fluff up my pillows for me would you?" Magda said, stretching. As Daphne plumped the pillows, she struggled to find the courage to ask Magda the question burning inside her.

"Miss Magellan," she bravely got out. "Am I really supposed to be wearing this uniform? Aren't I supposed to be your personal assistant?"

Magda stared coolly back. "If you want to be a star, you're going to have to start at the bottom and work your way up. Everyone must. You may hand me my breakfast tray now."

Daphne drew a determined breath. "Yes, Miss Magellan," she said.

By the end of her second week in Park Lane, Daphne felt exhausted. She'd soon found out she was only the latest in a long line of 'personal assistants'.

"It's the stairs," Mrs. Crunge had told her as they sat polishing Magda's vast store of silver knives, forks, spoons, coffee and teapots, candlesticks, ornaments and photograph frames. "Terrible thing this house is for stairs."

Silently, Daphne rubbed her aching calves. Mrs. C.

didn't need to tell her about the stairs. She'd been up and down them at least eight times today, and Magda hadn't even woken up yet.

First thing in the morning, moving quietly, Daphne carried up the heavy basket of wood for the fireplace in the sitting room next to Magda's luxurious bedroom, so the flames would be cheerfully leaping when she sat down later to do her telephoning. Magda loved chatting on the phone. She had friends all over the world and knew simply everyone in the entertainment business. Their names, addresses and telephone numbers were all carefully entered in the red leather address book she kept on her pretty antique desk. One of Daphne's many tasks was to keep the book up-to-date.

Next, Daphne collected from Mr. Crunge the pairs of shoes Magda had worn the day before, which he meticulously polished first thing each morning, and then returned to Magda's astonishing dressing room. "It looks like a warehouse!" Daphne had marvelled, when Mrs. Crunge had first shown her the room, which stretched along one whole side of the house and was fitted with elaborate lighting and mirrors.

"Madam never leaves the house without looking every inch a star, from her hat right down to her shoes," Mrs. Crunge said proudly.

The clothes were all laid out neatly on shelves and in drawers, or hung on racks in cupboards divided into sections — morning wear, afternoon wear, evening wear, suits, coats, furs, sporting wear, cruise wear, lingerie, shoes, handbags, hats and gloves. It was, of course, Daphne's job to preserve order in this realm of luxury. That meant washing and ironing in a never-ending river of maintenance, because Magda changed clothes several times a day.

After making sure the dressing room was in order, Daphne began her housework. First, more carrying of coal and wood to fireplaces throughout the house. There were ten in all, and they had to be ready to be lit at any hour of the day or night.

Next came a thorough clean and polish of Magda's bathroom. She had middle-of-the-night baths if she couldn't sleep after a performance, which she often followed by a night of dinner and dancing at one of London's hundreds of new nightclubs and cabarets.

The gold taps, shaped like dolphins, on the deep bathtub had to gleam. Piles of fluffy, snow-white towels had to be warmed on the heated towel rails. Tops had to be put back on the rows of lotions and perfumes, which lined the marble shelves. The scented white lilies, which were always kept in an etched glass vase by

Magda's make-up mirror, had to be freshly arranged each day.

After all of that, Daphne could sit down in the kitchen for a cup of tea, although it was usually interrupted by the ringing of Magda's breakfast bell. Back up the stairs Daphne went again with the tray.

After breakfast came Magda's bath, then Daphne's favourite time of the day, when she helped the star to dress and do her hair. That was when she and Magda talked. Although she was tight-fisted when it came to money, the star was lavishly generous in sharing her hard-won theatrical tips.

"You see, Daphne," she'd explained "doing make-up for real life and for the theatre are two completely different things. When I go out to lunch today I mustn't look as if I'm wearing much make-up at all. But, you see, on-stage, the audience has to be able to see your face clearly, even from the back row of the farthest balcony." She opened her make-up case and showed Daphne the rows of little pots of foundations, coloured creams and pencils, all specially made for stage work.

Of course, Magda always played heroines, but at the Royal Academy of Dramatic Art she'd learned how to do character make-up. "It's just like painting a portrait, but with your own face as the canvas," she demonstrated, drawing lines around her eyes and her mouth, which astonishingly, immediately made her look old and cruel. Daphne was enthralled. "This is very good for me, actually," Magda said, smiling. "It's just like dancing, you must always keep practising."

A lot of time was spent every day on Magda's famous hair, which she wore in many different styles. "I'm *almost* a real blonde, but sometimes, of course, a girl needs a weensy bit of help! You must promise me, Daphne, you'll keep all my tiny secrets," Magda had said in a voice that meant business.

"Of course, Miss Magellan," Daphne had replied, thinking she must be very careful indeed about what she told everyone in Hoxton, so as not to betray this sacred trust. Sometimes she let herself imagine she was Magda's younger sister, hearing about the backstage goings-on in Magda's current musical — who liked who and who couldn't really sing a note, although they thought they could!

Daphne could see Magda wasn't just interested in herself. There was a reason she had so many friends, and that was because she was a good friend herself and genuinely cared about what went on in other people's lives. As Daphne got to know her better she began to respect the fact that Magda's stardom hadn't gone to her head. Underneath the stupendous glamour she could still see traces of Maggie Morris from Shoreditch, who liked to put her feet up, have a good gossip and roar with laughter.

"Do tell me about that idiot Pettigrew again. Show me how she walked," she said, lounging gracefully in a chair while Daphne flicked her feather duster over the ornaments on the mantelpiece.

Assuming a posture of rigid grace, Daphne snarled, "Daphne Green, the letter S has a straighter spine than you've got," and watched with pleasure as Magda hooted with laughter.

It was at times like this that Daphne thought, *I LOVE this job*. Unfortunately, though, there were many more times when she thought, *I HATE this job*. Once Magda left for the theatre, driven by Crunge in her white Rolls-Royce, Daphne's work began in earnest.

She changed out of her black-and-white uniform and put on overalls of grey cotton, which always reminded her depressingly of her former St. Jude's uniform.

Once a week she had to thoroughly dust the chandeliers and the ceiling height paintings in the entrance hall. That meant struggling with a heavy ladder and scrambling up it, long-handled feather duster in hand, stretching to reach the topmost surfaces — stretching until her arms ached. In fact, all of her constantly ached — her knees, her arms, her legs and her back. *I'm never going to tell anyone what I do all day*, she thought, tight-lipped, as she polished the brass rails of the staircase to such a bright gleam her arms and wrists felt as if they were about to drop off.

She found it was becoming more and more difficult to keep her promise to herself to dance in every free hour she had. The warning she'd heard at Miss Pettigrew's was constantly in her thoughts. "A dancer who doesn't dance for two days loses his or her technique. A dancer who doesn't dance for a week is no longer a dancer." Now, with the grinding hours she worked as a maid, Daphne's only possible practise time was in the evening, after Magda had left for the theatre. But, most days, she felt far too tired to drag herself up to the attic, put on something she could dance in, and go downstairs to the ballroom. She knew she'd only have to go up again and change back into her uniform afterwards, because she had to be on hand to help her employer get undressed. If Magda wasn't home by midnight, Daphne could go to bed, up and up and up to her attic room, where the sound of the Crunges' dual snoring serenaded her from two doors down.

Frightened, she realised that her year was ticking

away: *three months gone already!* Suddenly she had a flash of inspiration. The scarlet stockings, might they be able to help her overcome her tiredness? There's no harm in trying was the last thought she had as, stiff and sore, she fell into an exhausted sleep.

As usual, the morning came much too soon. Daphne dragged herself out of bed when the alarm shrilled and dressed quickly. Then, carefully, she took the stockings from their tissue paper. They'd become even more precious to her the more unlikely it seemed that the goal she'd set for herself could be achieved.

As soon as they were on, the stockings immediately turned to black to match her uniform.

Daphne's heart sang a song of gratitude. The magic still worked! Usually she dragged herself down the stairs, rubbing her face to wake herself up. But this morning she ran lightly down the three flights; her calves didn't ache and her back didn't slump.

"GOOD morning," she said, bouncing into the kitchen.

"What's good about it? It's going to rain again and I've just washed the Rolls." Daphne ignored Crunge's pessimism. Underneath that gloomy exterior, he wasn't such a bad old stick.

"Let me help you, Mrs. Crunge," Daphne offered.

"I can bring the potatoes in from the pantry — it'll save your back."

"You're a good girl," Mrs. Crunge said, patting Daphne gratefully on the shoulder. "By far the best one we've had here, isn't she Crunge?" For a second a warm look passed over the butler's doom-laden features, but it quickly disappeared. "The last thing we need around here is another cheerful Charlie," he growled. He sat down, picked up the newspaper and snapped it open in front of his face before his wife could tell him off.

"I'm awfully sorry," Magda said later when Daphne brought in the breakfast tray with the morning post on it. "I'm afraid I left my letter opener downstairs. Would you mind getting it?"

"Not at all, Miss Magellan. I'll be back before you've even poured your first cup of tea." Daphne flew downstairs and was back in a flash with the slender pearl-handled knife.

"Goodness, Daphne, you look so happy this morning. Are you in love?" Magda asked hopefully. She loved hearing about romances.

She's had so many of her own, she must be absolutely dying to give me some advice, Daphne thought, smiling affectionately at her employer.

"I'm terribly sorry to disappoint you, Miss Magellan, but no I'm not."

"Pity," Magda said sympathetically, buttering her toast.

She must like me a bit, Daphne thought happily, *if she's asking me about my love life!*

For once, Daphne wished Magda would hurry up and leave for the theatre, where today she was to be interviewed for *Vogue* magazine. At last she was ready, "Do I look all right?" she asked, as Daphne closed the door of the Rolls.

"Beautiful, Miss Magellan, and your diamond clips look simply lovely on that dark green suit." Imagine! Magda Magellan seriously valued Daphne Green's opinion!

"Shameful flatterer!" Magda patted Daphne's hand, rolled up the car window and told Crunge to "Drive on." *Now for the housework*, Daphne thought eagerly.

What happened next was truly remarkable. She didn't puff, she didn't pant, she didn't wheeze, and she didn't grunt with effort. She flew from task to task, doing everything in a fraction of the time it usually took, as if the scarlet stockings were filling her with energy and putting springs on the soles of her feet.

After lunch, while the Crunges snoozed comfortably

in the armchairs by the kitchen hearth, Daphne went into the entrance hall and turned on all the chandeliers, ready for dusting. *This will be a real test*, she thought excitedly. *I'm going to see if I can do it without a ladder!* She positioned herself by the front door, muttered, "Run, run, LEAP!" and took off in a grand jeté that astonished her by its energy and height. As she passed the first chandelier, she swished her duster over it. Easy! With exhilaration, she repeated the manoeuvre until every last dangling pendant shone like a diamond.

Then suddenly, just as she was happily thinking, *I'm not only dusting, I'm dancing*, the chandeliers began behaving like maniacs.

First, they all turned themselves off at once. Then, although nothing else in the hall moved at all, they rattled deafeningly, their crystal drops clinking together, as if shaken by a violent earthquake. Next, they lit up in a random pattern of flashing lights, like an indoor firework display. And, at the same time as all of this was going on, the scarlet stockings began an urgent throbbing of their own, gaily shooting off little red flashes of energy in time with the pulsing chandeliers.

Daphne shrank back, staring down at her legs and clutching her feather duster to her. Then, as suddenly as it had all started, it stopped, leaving her shaking in a corner of the hall. *What on earth am I getting myself into*, she asked herself, dazed.

"Feeling all right, luv?" Mrs. Crunge asked her later that afternoon. "You've hardly said a word since lunchtime." Daphne just nodded, not trusting herself to reply.

She was sitting on a chair in the entrance hall, dozing, when her employer quietly let herself in at two a.m.

"Goodness, Daphne!" Magda said, clutching at her heart. "You gave me such a fright. Why aren't you in bed?" Chatting like the best of friends, they went upstairs. As Daphne undid the tiny buttons down the back of Magda's gold silk evening dress and put it carefully back onto its padded hanger, she noticed the star giving her a tentative smile.

"Daphne," she said. "I couldn't be more surprised, it's happened so quickly, but I find I really am getting extraordinarily fond of you. It must be because you're so exactly like I was at your age."

I wonder if I'll ever stop feeling grateful when somebody wants me, Daphne thought. What a wonderful ending to a most incredible day. And then it got even better.

The star knotted the belt of her dressing gown decisively. "You may call me Magda," she said.

Chapter Fifteen

The run of Magda's current hit musical had ended. She was now 'resting', as the theatrical term went. "I think I'll pop off and visit Mum for a few days," she told Daphne. "I haven't seen her for ages, and we do have such divine fun. We share the one teensy bedroom, but we don't sleep much because we're giggling rather a lot. The only thing is, I suppose I'll have to drag along that huge pile of scripts George is insisting I read. The man's more like an ogre than an agent! If it was up to him I'd never have a holiday at all!"

The good thing about Magda being away, Daphne thought, *is that I'll have some dancing time during the day. And all my evenings will be completely free.* She could feel the scarlet stockings gathering power, responding to the deepest wishes of her heart. Magda's stern remark about starting at the bottom was paying off. Daphne was thrilled to feel the developing strength of her back and muscles. And she noticed that her breathing and stamina were coming along nicely, too.

A few evenings after Magda had gone, Daphne was in the ballroom working hard on her solo fouettés. These were very difficult because, with no partner to support you, you had to spin repeatedly all the way round on one toe, whipping your leg out at each rotation to keep the movement going smoothly. She knew it was dangerous for her to be on pointe before a teacher said she could be. There was the possibility she might permanently damage her feet. But any really good ballet teacher would expect her to have progressed to pointe before they would take her on.

She had no choice but to trust in the scarlet stockings to keep her feet and ankles safe, she'd decided.

Tonight, she was so absorbed she didn't hear the door quietly opening. With a start, she heard the sound of clapping. She whirled around, "Magda! You're not supposed to be home until tomorrow."

"Darling, it was that unspeakable rooster. I simply couldn't take one more morning of him crowing his head off at dawn. I had to rush back to London for some peace and quiet! Terribly sorry to interrupt, but could you help me to change for dinner with my appalling agent? He telephoned me at Mum's about some frightful new show he wants me to do that will probably bore everyone to sobs!"

Putting on her mascara, Magda said casually over her shoulder to Daphne, "I was rather impressed with your dancing just now. Are you improving, would you say?"

"I think so, but it's terribly hard to tell without a teacher watching," Daphne said shyly.

Magda seemed to be thinking. "Go and tell Crunge I'm ready for the car, would you, darling? Oh, and bring me my telephone book, please."

Next morning, as Daphne brought in the breakfast tray, Magda sat up looking mischievous. "Are you terribly busy today?" she asked.

"Just the usual things."

"Oh, good, because there's a teensy errand I want you to run for me later." Daphne waited to hear what it was. "I telephoned Rudolf Gorky last night. He'll see you at five o'clock this afternoon."

It was a good thing Daphne had already laid the tray across Magda's lap, or else there would be broken china and spilled milk all over the white bedroom carpet.

"Rudolf Gorky! He taught Ova Andova. He's the most famous ballet teacher outside Russia."

"Goodness, you look as if you're going to faint. You'd

better sit down on the bed," Magda advised, smiling. "I told him, in my view, he should see you for his class. It's my professional opinion that, at this stage in your career, you should be properly taught."

Loving Magda for referring to her 'career' as if they were equals, Daphne said, her heart sinking, "Oh, but I couldn't possibly afford Mr. Gorky's classes."

Magda waved an airy hand. "Let's call it a loan. The same kind of loan George Cardew made to me."

"Magda," Daphne said in a voice she hardly recognised as her own. "I insist that you put down that cup of tea. I must hug you and I must hug you NOW!"

"Funny little thing!" Magda said, holding out her arms. "Now, pop along and run my bath, would you, darling?"

While Magda was bathing, Daphne tore up the stairs to get the scarlet stockings to take them to her sewing room for a quick wash. Leaving them to dry draped over her ironing board, she darted across the corridor into the kitchen to tell the Crunges her wonderful news.

Surprisingly, Crunge offered, "I'll ask Madam if she needs the car this afternoon. If she doesn't, I'll ask her if I can drive you to Soho for your audition."

"Thank you, Mr. Crunge, that's terribly kind of you," she said, touched.

Magda came into the kitchen in her dressing gown.

"You're excused housework for today, Daphne," she said. "I think you'd better go and practise."

So, gratefully, Daphne did. She was so absorbed, she was nearly late, and just had time to rush upstairs and change into a leotard and tights. Wages well-spent, she thought, standing on her bed so she could see herself in the little mirror over her chest of drawers. The ballet shop had allowed her to give a deposit on her two pairs of pointe shoes, and said she could pay the rest off in instalments.

She flew down to the sewing room to get the scarlet stockings. It was quiet in the house. Magda had gone out for cocktails, Mrs. Crunge was at the shops, and Crunge was getting the car.

In a rush, Daphne opened the door of her sewing room.

And her heart almost stopped beating.

THE SCARLET STOCKINGS WERE GONE!

She got down on her knees, praying to see a flash of scarlet on the floor. But there was nothing. Frantically she checked every cupboard and drawer. Again, horribly, nothing.

She heard Crunge calling her from the kitchen. *I'll have to go*, Daphne thought in a panic. Rudolf Gorky was well known for turning people away who arrived even one minute late for class. She allowed herself a faint hope. Perhaps she wasn't supposed to wear the stockings today? Perhaps the magic was testing her to see if she'd been working hard enough, and wanted her to manage on her own?

Shakily, she joined Crunge in the front seat of the Rolls. At any other time, her eyes would have been out on stalks as he manoeuvred the big car through Soho's narrow streets, with their exotic restaurants, fascinating shops selling costumes and dancewear, and seedy doorways leading down to questionable nightclubs. But, with her stomach in knots, Daphne hardly looked up. The only sight that briefly captured her attention was the Berwick Street market with its fruit and vegetable stalls, a miniature version of Hoxton's. It brought her a brief moment of comfort.

The Rolls stopped in front of a narrow building. Over its big second story windows was a painted sign reading, '**Rudolf Gorky Studio of Dance**'. Daphne clutched her stomach. She felt sick with nerves.

Crunge pointed across the street to a rundown café with grimy lace curtains at its windows. "I'll wait for you over there. If it's thumbs down, we'll order ourselves two nice cups of tea with arsenic!" Daphne managed a faint smile.

The faces of the dancers streaming out of the building gave her a shock. Until now she'd only seen them in newspaper and magazine photographs. Feeling her knees tremble, she climbed the stairs to an airy room, where a thin, elegant white-haired man dressed all in black greeted her.

"Ah," he said. "You must be the girl Magda insisted I see. And your name again?"

"Daphne Green," she managed to get out through her frozen lips.

"Well, Miss Green, I will watch you dance and give you my opinion as to whether you have the talent Magda believes you have. I understand you have taught yourself to dance?" Daphne nodded speechlessly. "Not an encouraging start, but one which could possibly be overcome in time." Daphne remembered she'd heard almost exactly these words before from Miss Pettigrew. And look what had happened then!

Gorky took pity on her frightened face. "Prepare and let me see your warm-ups," he said gently.

Daphne took her place at the barre. *Monsieur Beauchamp promised magic*, she thought desperately. *But can I trust him?*

Half an hour later, the door of the café opened and Daphne came listlessly in. "Arsenic?" Crunge asked sympathetically, squeezing her cold hand. Daphne looked at him in hopeless misery.

"It's all right. I'll take you home," Crunge said. Their drive back to Park Lane took place in silence.

When they got there, Mrs. Crunge was sitting in front of the kitchen fire. "Madam won't be in for dinner," she began, then she stopped short as she saw Daphne's face. "Oh, dear," she said. "Bad, was it, then?"

Daphne flung herself down at the kitchen table. "I was worse than bad, I was ordinary. I know I could have done better if I hadn't been so horribly nervous."

"What did the teacher say, luv?" Mrs. Crunge asked softly.

"He doesn't want me," Daphne whispered.

Chapter Sixteen

It was shortly after half past eight the next morning when Rudolf Gorky arrived at his studio. He almost tripped over a huddled figure on the doorstep. The huddle stood up, quickly whipped off its coat to show the dance clothes underneath, and said nervously, "Do you remember me from yesterday, Mr. Gorky? I'm Daphne Green. I work for Magda Magellan."

"I remember you."

"I'm so ashamed of my audition for you. I was terrified. I can do much, much better. Please let me show you."

And before the ballet teacher could draw a breath to refuse, Daphne began dancing along the pavement, using all the most difficult steps she'd learned. Her fouettés were so fast she was almost a blur. Passers-by stopped to watch the extraordinary sight and call out encouragement.

"Don't see that every day, do you?" a woman said

loudly and appreciatively as Daphne came to a panting halt.

Gorky gave Daphne a thin smile. "I see," he said. "Please assure me that this is the last time you will dance on pointe on paving stones. Your feet are your most precious asset."

Later that morning, Magda was surprised to find it was Mrs. Crunge who was opening her bedroom curtains. "Where's Daphne?" she asked, worried. "I hope the disappointment about Gorky hasn't made her ill."

"No, Madam, but I think one of her family in Hoxton might be. She left a note on the kitchen table saying it was five o'clock this morning and she'd had to go somewhere for an emergency. She said she hoped to be back in time to bring up your breakfast tray, as usual." Light feet sounded on the stairs. "That must be her now."

Daphne danced into Magda's bedroom in her ballet clothes and on pointe. "I'm a ballerina! Or at least I will be when Mr. Gorky's finished with me!"

"Daphne!" Magda shouted happily. "How did you pull it out of the hat, you clever, clever girl?" Then, she and Mrs. Crunge hung on every word of Daphne's rapid explanation.

"You mustn't let your tea and toast get cold, Magda.

I'll just go up and change quickly so I'll be ready to help you get dressed," Daphne said, unable to stop smiling.

When she came back downstairs again, she found Magda in her dressing room, looking puzzled. "Did you put these here, Daphne? I've never seen them before."

Mrs. Crunge bustled in with the shoes Crunge had just finished polishing.

"I did, Madam," she said. "I thought they must be part of one of your costumes."

"They're mine, actually," Daphne said. *Thank goodness, oh thank goodness my practising is working,* she thought jubilantly.

And she took the scarlet stockings from Magda's outstretched hand.

In Hoxton the following Sunday, the tea party at the Greens' was in full swing. The dear, familiar faces of Daphne's audience wore identical expressions of suspense.

"So then, Mr. Gorky said I'd better come upstairs and dance properly for him, so I did and he said YES!"

"You must have been practising non-stop. No wonder we haven't seen hide nor hair of you since you left," Dolly said, beaming her congratulations.

"I'm terribly sorry I haven't been home." She turned

to Carlo and Maria. "It's just that I'm desperate to show you it wasn't a mistake to let me go to Park Lane, and my job with Magda turned out to be much busier than I'd expected. I had to use my Sundays off to dance."

"You call her Magda, now?" Lofty asked, awed.

"Well, she asked me to, and you can't imagine how much fun she is. We talk about everything, and she said she's dying to come and meet you all," Daphne said. Her remark produced a general gasp of amazement. Magda Magellan in Hoxton! Actually sitting in the Greens' parlour!

"So then what happened?" Joe asked eagerly.

"Mr. Gorky said he was going to telephone Magda and tell her she'd have to find someone else to do the housework, because he couldn't have me coming to class too exhausted to lift a leg," Daphne said, laughing.

"Heavens!" Lofty said. "How did she take that?"

"I was with her when he rang up, and the darling got all huffy and told him of course she had no intention of making me polish windows now I was going to be a ballerina, what kind of an idiot did he think she was!" Daphne frowned anxiously. "I do worry all the time about when I'll ever be able to repay her for my lessons, but she swears she doesn't mind."

Magda, had, in fact, surprised Daphne and the Crunges

by telling them she was giving them all a raise. "I don't know quite why it is," she'd told Daphne, "but for some peculiar reason I'm not as worried about money these days as I used to be. I've always been absolutely terrified it would all disappear. I must say it's a huge relief!"

Daphne had thought, wonderingly, how *real* worries could seem. Like hers when she was so frightened the Greens wouldn't like her. How amazing! Even the beautiful, famous Magda Magellan had her secret fears!

"Anyway, Mrs. Crunge has hired two girls, Elsie and Pansy, to replace me," she continued. "They're really nice, they sleep in the bedroom next to mine." She stopped for a breath and a bite of her egg-and-tomato sandwich. "Mmm, delicious, Mum." She ached to tell them about how the scarlet stockings had been helping her, but, of course, she couldn't breathe a word. She smiled to herself. *They'd think I'd gone mad, anyway!*

"The good thing is that, now I'm taking Mr. Gorky's classes from Monday to Saturday, I don't need to use all my spare time on Sundays for practise. So I'll be able to come home every week," Daphne said happily.

She beamed round at Joe and Lofty and Dolly. "What are the Friends up to, and have you still got room for a dancer?"

★ ★ ★

At the Gorky Studio of Dance, Daphne's classmates were stunned at her progress. She'd even overheard the envious word *prodigy* used. Each day, Daphne took group classes with a variety of the studio's teachers, until, in the late afternoon, after all the other dancers had left, she began her gruelling private classes with Gorky himself. Each night, going home on the omnibus sore and limp, longing only for bed, she blessed Magda for her generosity. *Perhaps I'll never have to wear a school uniform again*, Daphne told herself hopefully.

That seed of hope became a seedling when Rudolf Gorky told her she was worth all the extra work he was putting into her, and that her progress was remarkable.

For the first time in her life, Daphne was beginning to be proud of herself.

But one thing hadn't changed. She still felt in awe of her famous teacher. Rudolf Gorky was a perfectionist, brusquely intolerant of any weakness shown. Illness or tiredness cut no ice with him. "When you dance you leave everything else at the door," he barked at her one morning when she showed up with a touch of early summer flu. "The curtain will go up regardless of how you are feeling. Never forget that every talented dancer has a string of others behind them waiting to take their place if he or she falters or fails."

Now, on this soft summer evening, Daphne sat on the studio floor, anxiously examining her bare feet. She noticed the calluses she'd developed on the balls of them and on her toes were getting ready to open up and bleed again. Gloomily, she returned her new pointe shoes to her dance bag. They'd given her an agonising bruise, even though she'd banged them on a wall and shut them in a door a few times to soften them up. She would have to sit with her feet in a basin of warm water and Epsom salts again before going to bed.

The rehearsal pianist had gone home. Only she and Gorky were left in the studio. He was looking at her with a strange expression, half smiling, half stern. Now, he was walking over to her, holding out a square envelope. Daphne tore it open. All the colour drained out of her face.

ANNUAL AUDITIONS

Ballet Splendide de Paris

August 24th, 1923, from 10 – 6 o'clock

NO. 29

She felt so faint she had to put her head down between her knees before she could whisper, "Does this mean what I think it does, Mr. Gorky?"

With one of his rare smiles, the teacher replied, "Although I would have sworn it was impossible when I first saw you dance, you have worked with energy and discipline. I believe you are ready to try for this opportunity. I have spoken to my friend and colleague Serge Petrov, the director general of the Splendide, and he has agreed to include you in this year's audition."

Daphne's head shot up. Andova's teacher thought she was ready. Her heart beat even faster. Perhaps Andova herself would attend the auditions! Daphne looked again at the card in her trembling hand. "But that's in two weeks!"

"You are correct," Gorky replied drily. "And so, Miss Green, we shall be extremely busy until then. We must increase the number of our private classes."

Daphne stared ferociously at her calluses, willing them with all her might not to cripple her before then.

At Victoria Station, the morning train, connecting with the cross-Channel steamer to France, puffed out steam like an overheated dragon. The grey swirls floated higher and higher, up past the metal girders to the glass skylights of the roof. Daphne, dressed with Parisian chic, busily created by Dolly between one of Daphne's Sunday visits and the next, leaned out of her carriage's open window toward the three Friends on the platform below.

"Telephone us at the Cheadles on Sunday as soon as you get the news," Joe said. "We'll be waiting there at noon, on tenterhooks."

The guard's whistle shrilled. "All aboard, ladies and gentlemen, if you please." He walked along the platform, slamming the carriage doors shut.

"Here," Dolly said, handing up a dog-eared copy of *Vogue*. "Ma saved it for you for the train."

"These are for you, too," Lofty said, presenting Daphne with a bunch of white roses from the market, with the dew still on them. "I hope you're not too nervous."

In fact, Daphne had woken up feeling so terrified that, for reassurance, she'd put on the scarlet stockings when dressing in her travelling clothes. Now, her heart thumped as Lofty said the word *nervous*. Was her fear of being good enough showing? How babyish. It mustn't. She couldn't let it. She felt the stockings, which had been as cold as her own hands, suddenly turning fiery hot, as if resenting the implication that she, magic's own child, might not be quite up to it when it came to the audition.

She found herself replying haughtily, "Not at all, I expect I'll do very well."

The whistle blew again and the train chugged away, leaving three very puzzled people on the platform.

"That didn't sound like Daphne," Lofty said.

"Didn't you think she sounded like a real show-off?" Dolly asked bluntly.

Loyally, Joe spoke up on his adopted sister's behalf. "Probably just over-rehearsal," he said, trying not to look as surprised and worried as he felt.

Chapter Seventeen

Completely unaware of having ruffled any feathers, Daphne settled back into her seat. She began to rehearse her audition in her head, tapping out the rhythms of the variations on her knee.

In the afternoon, after the boat and another train, French this time, Daphne arrived in Paris. It was the oddest thing. As soon as her feet touched the pavements she felt at home. "Hôtel Mouffetard, s'il vous plaît," she said in her best St. Jude's French accent to the taxi driver. The hotel was on the Left Bank of the River Seine, close to the Théâtre Splendide and its rehearsal rooms. Magda had suggested it and booked it for Daphne.

Daphne paused in the hotel lobby only long enough to see it was pretty and charming, before leaving her small suitcase and running out into the beckoning streets, with their new sights, sounds, and smells. Fantastic Paris! *It feels as if something exciting and romantic could happen here any minute!*

Happily wandering the tree-lined streets, she found herself at sunset at the white-domed Sacré Coeur church on top of its hill. Sitting on a marble bench, she watched, enthralled, as the sun set over the jumble of Paris's old rooftops. In the dusky blue twilight, a carpet of diamond lights twinkled into life below her. *I'll die if I don't get into the Splendide*, she thought fiercely.

She had a wretched night and hardly slept at all. When she did, she dreamed of turning up tomorrow for her audition without the scarlet stockings. At last daylight came. Shivering in the early morning chill, she opened the windows and threw back the clanging metal shutters of her hotel room. The pleasant clinking sounds of breakfast being served, and the smell of fresh coffee, drifted up from the pretty courtyard below. The coffee's strong aroma brought nervous bile to her mouth. *I hate how I always feel sick when I'm scared*, she thought miserably. *But I'll have to force myself to eat something, or I'll dance like a wilted old piece of St. Jude's cabbage.*

The morning sun warmed her cold, nervous body as she sat at her table in a quiet corner of the courtyard. She felt better after her bowl of milky coffee, dish of strawberries and hot, flaky croissant. But the butterflies in her stomach resumed their wild flamenco as the nice hotel receptionist drew her a little map, showing her the way to the Place Splendide. "Bonne chance, good luck, Mademoiselle," he wished her with a fatherly smile.

Magda had told her that, in August, except for tourists, Paris's streets would probably be quiet, because the Parisians themselves all left the city then for their summer holidays. It was wonderfully calming, walking along the peaceful, sun-dappled pavements to where the massive Théâtre Splendide stood, taking up one whole side of a big circular plaza with a spectacular fountain in the middle of it.

Daphne found her way to the Splendide's stage door, and collected her No. 29 sash from the French version of Tom. He had a nice smile like Tom's, too. He introduced himself as Edouard and pointed the way to the wings. Her knees shaking, Daphne joined the other young male and female dancers warming up. Tying the ribbons of her ballet shoes, she silently begged the scarlet stockings, *please help me to do my best*. As if in friendly response, she felt their reassuring, energising heat.

A short, dark-haired man with a crumpled, amusing face climbed up on-stage from the auditorium and announced that he was Monsieur Philippe, the

Splendide's ballet master. "Mademoiselles and messieurs," he said, "the auditions will now begin. I hope you have all had time to complete your warm-ups. When your number is called, please hand your music to the pianist and take your position."

Craning from the wings, Daphne saw an imposingly elegant man, unmistakably the director general, Serge Petrov, seated in the fourth row of the stalls, surrounded by his teaching staff. The auditions began. With mounting panic, Daphne admired the excellence of each dancer. But how very nerve-racking it all was. Nobody applauded; there was nothing but the ballet master's quiet "thank you" each time someone bowed or curtseyed, collected their music, and left the stage. Then, after a short pause for consultation with his colleagues, Petrov's deep, unemotional voice called, "Next."

"Number twenty-nine." With freezing, trembling fingers, Daphne touched the stockings and walked to the piano. With the music's introductory bars, she breathed deeply, calling up all the times she'd rehearsed this exact moment with Rudolf Gorky. Then she began, giving herself over completely to the melody and the rhythm, calling on her heart to portray the passion she felt, the love of the variations she was performing.

She was dancing perfectly, instinctively, as, running, she soared in a grand jeté, her mind so focused she was completely unaware that Petrov was leaning over, murmuring something to the efficient-looking secretary at his side, notepad in hand.

Shockingly, at the very height of her leap, the auditorium's doors crashed open. The loud, echoing BANG brought Daphne down to earth in a landing so ungraceful that she stumbled and almost fell. *Oh, no, I've ruined it,* she wailed to herself. The music came to an abrupt stop. Daphne stood frozen at the centre of the stage.

A furious slender figure, dressed in practise clothes so stylish they must have come from one of Paris's finest couturiers, stormed down the aisle. "Serge, I will not stand for this a moment longer," she screeched. "Your new rehearsal pianist is a dolt. He is telling me it is I who am not knowing the music."

Petrov stood up with weary exasperation. "Ova, please. Can you not see we are auditioning?"

"Pah!" the prima ballerina *assoluta* spat out disdainfully. "These are people of no importance. It is only my happiness that should be concerning you. I insist you dismiss that idiot. Today!"

"Make a note, Miss Tripp," Petrov said, his teeth

gritted. "I will look into it, Ova. Now, would you have the goodness to return to your rehearsal."

"TODAY, Serge." Andova flounced away.

Petrov sighed deeply and sat down again. "You may begin again, Mademoiselle," he said.

"Sit down, lad, you're making me nervous," Carlo growled at Joe next day in the Cheadle's front parlour.

"I'd like to walk up and down with 'im," Maria said, wringing her hands. "Why 'asn't she telephoned? It's almost one o'clock." Everyone stared at the squat bulk of the telephone.

"They were probably late posting the notices, Mrs. G," Dolly said, stitching furiously at a piece of mending.

"Cup of tea?" Sheila asked, coming in with a loaded tray. "To pass the time, like." There was a lot of silent sipping. Suddenly the telephone sprang into life with a raucous *brrring, brrring.* "Someone else'll 'ave to get it," Sheila said, clutching her heart. "Me legs 'ave gone like wet noodles."

Joe strode across the room and lifted the receiver. "Joe Green speaking," he said firmly. He turned to Harry Cheadle. "It's the Paris operator. She wants to know if we'll accept the call." At Harry's nod, Joe spoke again into the phone. "Yes, we will, operator." He stood, tapping his foot impatiently, waiting for Daphne to come on the line.

"Hello, luv," he said after a moment. Daphne was obviously chattering on about Paris, squeezing all the drama she could out of the situation, because Joe suddenly yelled, "Well? TELL US!"

"She says to say *bonjour* to the newest member of the Ballet Splendide!" he shouted triumphantly.

The ensuing noise of people jumping up and down, cheering and thumping each other on the back, could be heard clearly at the other end of the line by Daphne in Paris.

PART THREE

'Choosing, you will test me.'

Chapter Eighteen

The apartment Daphne had found in Paris's ancient Rue des Arts was on the third floor of an old building painted in a faded pale yellow. It was only streets away from the Théâtre Splendide, and right around the corner from the historic Marché Mouffetard. She'd sent a postcard to Dolly, writing on the back, *You'd love this market, Doll. Can you believe it, at weekends they have accordion players!*

The tiny apartment had only two rooms, a small bedroom, and a larger main room with a primitive kitchen at one end of it. There was an equally primitive bathroom off the little hall where the front door was. But Daphne was thrilled. It was hers. One of the waiters at the Hôtel Mouffetard had told her it was for rent. His sister had been living there, but she was getting married and moving with her new husband to Avignon. "Do you think I might get it?" Daphne had asked him. "Because I've only got a week to find somewhere and move in before I start at the Splendide." The waiter had assured her he'd make certain his sister put in a good word for her.

After Daphne signed the lease, she spent a few whirlwind days practising her French by acquiring some simple furniture from the district's many little second-hand shops. *Thank goodness the French word for table is 'table'*, she thought, ruefully. Sister P's dreaded French classes seemed long ago and far away now, but amazingly they'd been of use after all! As a symbolic peacemaking gesture with her old enemy, Daphne bought a little china hedgehog she'd spotted in a shop window, and put it into position on her mantelpiece. "J'aime bien les herissons, j'aime bien les herissons, j'aime bien les herissons!" she said to it.

As she stood arranging a bunch of market roses in a pretty, chipped turquoise vase, again Daphne blessed Magda's generosity. The furniture, sheets, towels, and dishes for the Rue des Arts had all been paid for from a wad of notes Magda had insisted on pushing into her hand when Daphne had gone to say goodbye to everyone in Park Lane. "For life's little necessities, darling. And perhaps just a few teensy luxuries! And of course my chum Marie-Hélène from the Comédie Française will be popping around to keep an eye on you," Magda added, casually naming the adored leading actress at France's national theatre.

For a penny, Daphne had picked up an old glass jar. She'd stuck a label on it reading MAGELLAN REPAYMENT FUND, and vowed to put in it a quarter of every week's salary.

At twilight, watching Paris's lights come on from her very own terrace, Daphne breathed a silent prayer of thanks to Pierre Beauchamp.

The next morning, she stood in front of a discreet brass plaque, engraved '**Ballet Splendide, Rehearsal Rooms and Offices**'. *This* was what she'd dreamed of, what she'd worked for until she'd watched the blood seeping painfully through the pink satin of her ballet shoes.

Other dancers were arriving now, laughing and chattering, and Daphne was swept along with them. In the wide entrance corridor inside the stage door hung a series of blackboards, chalked with the daily timetable for the more than one hundred dancers who made up the Splendide's company.

Feeling intimidated and bewildered by the complicated lists of dance, movement, and acting classes, rehearsals and costume fittings, Daphne searched until, with a shiver of pride, she found her own name and read she was scheduled to begin in an hour with a movement class. Next to the blackboards were the lists of dressing room assignments. Daphne was in 'Corps de Ballet 2'.

She was just about to ask someone for directions when she heard a commotion at the stage door. In swept Andova, star quality crackling electrically around her. Her dresser, Grushka, creaked along in her wake like a battered rowboat trailing a sleek transatlantic liner. Rudely, the *assoluta* pushed her way through the crowd by the noticeboards. The dancers were too lowly to greet. She ignored them all. To Edouard she said, "My letters, doorman."

"Can't be bothered to remember my name after all this time," Edouard muttered angrily to himself. But he answered politely, "The post has not yet arrived, Madame, but it should be here at any moment."

Andova looked viciously around, then jerked her thumb at Daphne. "You", she said, "the new girl, you shall be waiting here and you will be bringing it to my dressing room."

Daphne flushed nervously.

Never is it too soon to show these young upstarts how insignificant they are, Andova thought grimly, sweeping away.

"You don't have to, you know," Edouard told Daphne. "It is not your job, it is the job of the call-boy to run errands."

"Dear, adorable Ova, up to her old tricks," one of the male dancers said to Daphne. "Be careful, she's poison."

"I don't mind doing it. I'd like to see her dressing room, I've seen pictures," she replied, shyly.

The boy shrugged. "Watch out!" he warned.

Within a few minutes the postman arrived, whistling, and handed Edouard a stack of letters and packages. He quickly riffled through them before handing Daphne the ones for Andova. "These seem the most important," he said. "All the rest looks like fan mail. Like it or not, Her Royal Highness will just have to wait until I've sorted those out later!"

Knocking on the door of Dressing Room no.1, Daphne heard Grushka's voice brusquely telling her to enter. And even though she thought she knew what to expect, Daphne was still astounded. The photographs she'd seen didn't begin to do justice to the room's extraordinary richness and luxury.

The faded floor tiles had been covered with the most sumptuous of rugs, hand woven by the nomadic tribes of the Russian steppes. The cracked plaster walls had disappeared under their enormous portraits of Andova in her most famous roles – doomed Giselle, the Lilac Fairy in *Sleeping Beauty*, the mechanical doll *Coppelia*, and, of course, the role in which Daphne had seen and adored her, Odette/Odile in *Swan Lake*. All the plain light bulbs had been removed and replaced with soft pink ones. The star's daybed, carved in the shape of a swan and smothered in furs, had once belonged to an empress. The air smelled deliciously of her special perfume, Ova.

Since Andova didn't acknowledge her presence by so much as a flicker of her eyelids, Daphne worked out she must be deliberately ignoring her, giving her time to be duly impressed. *Well, I AM*, she thought, as intimidated as it seemed the star meant her to be. At last, regally, the *assoluta* held out her hand for the letters. As soon as Daphne handed them over, Andova made a vicious hissing noise and fixed her with a despising stare. "Go, creature," she said, with a contemptuous dismissing gesture.

Daphne flinched. *I don't really belong here, and everyone will soon know it*, she anguished. Turning abruptly on her heel, before the *assoluta* could see the shame on her face, Daphne stumbled from the room.

The stockings put an immediate end to her self-doubt.

She heard a sound like waves crashing on a shore. Her pale pink dance tights suddenly changed colour, rolling up her legs encouragingly over and over again in rhythmic waves of scarlet. *I DO belong here*, Daphne told herself, her heart leaping with renewed hope and confidence. *I've earned my place in this company.*

As the scarlet waves and the ocean's roar gradually receded, she pulled herself together. *I'll have to get a lot tougher*, she told herself, frowning. *That must be what the riddle meant by* **Choosing, you will test me**. *It'll be up to me whether I let Andova crush me.*

Choosing, you will test me. Her shoulders stiffened. It was a test she mustn't fail, on peril of death.

Inside Dressing Room no.1, Ova snarled to Grushka, "This one is trouble. I feel it and I am never wrong." She peered, frowning, into her make-up mirror. Those lines around her eyes and mouth were certainly getting deeper.

"No one can dance like you," Grushka soothed.

"Pah!" Ova replied viciously. "I am knowing what to do. I am doing it many times before. Soon that one will be wishing she had never *heard* the word, *arabesque.*"

Grushka snickered. Then, brushing Ova's gleaming hair with long, firm strokes, she said approvingly, "She would be proud of you today."

The 'she' referred to was Ova's role model, her dazzling, fascinating Aunt Violetta, who had lived in Russia in splendour, gained by the patronage of a string of admirers whose names were too famous to say out loud. Aunt Violetta had never cared what anyone had thought of her. Ignoring every rule of good taste, she'd blazed through St. Petersburg like a comet. Everything about her loudly proclaimed her own name. Her hair, her clothes, the décor of her fabulous house the size of a small palace, all were in shades of violet. Her carriage, drawn by a superb pair of white horses, decked out in mauve harnesses and ostrich plumes, had been repainted no less than fourteen times to achieve the exact shade of violet she wanted.

As a child, the only member of her large family to inherit her aunt's sensational violet eyes, Ova was, naturally, her favourite niece. At unpredictable intervals the famous beauty would swoop down on the boring provincial town where Ova and her family lived, bearing gifts worthy of a princess. By the time she was six, Ova possessed a vast doll's house modelled on the Russian royal family's blue, white, and gold Summer Palace, a doll's tea service custom-made by the famous English porcelain company Royal Derby, and an extensive wardrobe of handmade clothes and lace-trimmed silk underwear. Ova would sit for hours at Violetta's feet, entranced by the aroma of perfume and the clashing of gold bracelets.

At the age of five, she heard from her aunt the words which would rule Ova's own life: "When you are seeing something you are wanting, you are *not* waiting, you are going *straight* for it." This advice fell on receptive ears. The young Ova's tantrums were legendary. She got whatever she wanted by the simple method of throwing something breakable as hard as she could against a wall, and screaming until she turned – well, violet!

Although in every other way Ova was a nightmare of selfishness and pride, loathed by everyone except her dotingly indulgent nanny, Grushka, the fairies leaning over her cradle at birth had given her one redeeming feature. She could dance. Oh, how she could dance, like a gossamer wisp of thistledown, like a snow-flake shimmering to earth, like an angel. As soon as this talent became obvious, Aunt Violetta swooped down for the last time and removed Ova and her nanny, Grushka, permanently to Russia's capital city, St. Petersburg.

No one, it must honestly be said, was sorry to see her go.

At the age of ten, following years of private lessons, Aunt Violetta enrolled her in the finest ballet school in the world, the Imperial Ballet Academy. Ova graduated eight years later, an instrument of artistic and creative perfection. Her scheming personality remained loathsome, and she became famously known for her invariable behaviour: 'Be very, very difficult and then say NO!' But her talent was unrivalled, and within five years she became the reigning star of St. Petersburg's famous Mariinsky Theatre. European tours followed. For the past ten years she had been the prima ballerina *assoluta* of the Splendide, reputedly paid a fortune by Serge Petrov, whose business sense, like Andova's tantrums and her dancing, was legendary.

While Ova was preening, Daphne found her own third-floor dressing room. It was an almost laughable contrast to the one she'd just left, dingy and echoing, filled with a row of wooden tables, topped by mirrors surrounded by bare light bulbs. The smell of sweat and talcum powder hung in the air. The long room was filled with the loud chatter of twenty girls changing into their exercise clothes and setting out their stage make-up.

Daphne found her labelled drawer and chair and sat down to unpack her dance bag. The drawer was deep and lockable with its own small key. Making sure no one was watching her, Daphne slid in *The Scarlet Stockings* script. She wanted it always close to her while she was dancing. She locked the drawer, pocketed the key, and decided she'd keep it comfortingly strung around her neck under her clothes. *Even though I'm the youngest dancer at the Splendide, I've got magic on my side,* she thought, locking the script away.

The blonde girl seated next to her, pulling back her long hair in front of the mirror, turned and smiled. "Sophie de la Faisanderie," she said, holding out her hand and waiting pleasantly for Daphne to introduce herself.

I wish I had a name like that. Mine's so boring and lower-class, Daphne thought enviously. She ignored a little voice inside her saying that, not only was the thought disgustingly snobbish, but it would have hurt the Greens' feelings very much if they'd known she was thinking it. "Daphne Green," she told Sophie. "But I'm probably changing it."

Sophie introduced her to some of the other girls in the corps de ballet, but Daphne hardly heard their names — Francoise, Alice, Natasha — because she was obsessively dreaming of one day having a dressing room as luxurious as Andova's.

★ ★ ★

As the weeks went by, it became obvious to everyone that the prima ballerina *assoluta* loathed Daphne. She humiliated her with constant criticism in class, insisting that Daphne dance alongside her to see how it was done. Of course, Andova always made sure that these were variations she'd performed a hundred times, while Daphne was only just learning them. "Clumsy, awkward," Andova could then say to the room in general. And she 'accidentally' didn't see Daphne while complaining loudly to the director general about how miserably untalented the new company members he'd hired were, especially the little English girl.

"Don't let her break your spirit, that's what she's after. She's doing it because she knows you're good," Sophie said furiously as Daphne wept buckets after one particularly vicious class.

Later that night, Daphne lay bleakly awake, her thoughts cold and steely. *Choosing, you will test me. I WILL fulfil my destiny, no matter who or what gets in my way. Rudolf Gorky was right. If I'm living in a cut-throat world, then I'll have to be just as cut-throat.*

That wasn't what Rudolf Gorky had either said or meant, but Daphne had no trouble convincing herself that it was. For the first time in her life she was actually grateful to the orphanage because it had taught her never to show weakness, to trust nobody.

It was then that the fragile part of Daphne, the part that had opened and flowered in Hoxton, snapped its petals closed again.

Next day, she strode into class and, as she dipped the soles of her ballet shoes in the box of powdered rosin, there to prevent the dancers from slipping, she muttered furiously to herself and to the scarlet stockings, "We'll show them, we'll just show them what we can do."

That afternoon, Monsieur Philippe tapped on the door of Petrov's office. "Come." The impresario looked up from his enormous desk, covered with papers, costume sketches, and miniature set models. "You wished to see me?"

"It is about this year's production of *The Nutcracker.* We are casting it now, yes?" the ballet master said.

"We are, with Andova as usual as the Sugar Plum Fairy," Petrov agreed. "One of our biggest money-makers, and this year it must succeed even above our expectations, my friend. I am counting on the income for some badly needed refurbishments."

"That's why I have come to ask you to attend class this afternoon. We must decide who will dance the part of Clara. In my opinion —"

"Your invaluable opinion," Petrov interrupted.

Philippe smiled warmly at his long-time colleague. "I believe our best choice is to take Alice Durocher out of the corps de ballet. It's always good to show our younger dancers that, if they work hard, they will be rewarded."

"How long has the girl been with us?"

"This is her third year."

"Very well, I'll attend your class and watch her dance," the impresario said. Later that day, Petrov quietly entered and took a seat at the back of the rehearsal room, watching intently. Although it was too soon to give her an important role, that new girl, Magda Magellan's protégée, had an almost supernatural technique, he thought shrewdly. He wondered if her character was as interesting as her face. He would make time to find out.

The class came to a close and the dancers made their reverence to Petrov and Philippe. The two men knew each other so well that all Petrov had to do was to nod at the ballet master in confirmation of his choice of Alice Durocher for *The Nutcracker's* young heroine, Clara. Returning to his office, he buzzed for his efficient secretary, Miss Tripp.

"Please tell Alice Durocher I wish to see her here at nine o'clock tomorrow morning. And tell Daphne Green I wish to interview her half an hour later."

Chapter Nineteen

Miss Tripp was having a very busy day, but she stopped what she was doing and went looking for the two girls. She found Daphne after a tedious twenty-minute search. "Mademoiselle Green," she said briskly, "the director general wishes to see you at half past nine tomorrow morning in his office."

Daphne went white. *What have I done wrong?* she agonised.

Miss Tripp glanced at her watch. She'd spent enough time on these young dancers. "You share a dressing room with Alice Durocher, I believe?" Daphne nodded. "Then please tell her that Monsieur Petrov wants to see her first, at nine," she said, hurrying away.

Daphne went slowly into an empty rehearsal room and sat down on a folding chair. Instinctively, her hands moved to stroke the stockings. *I don't think I've done anything terrible*, she thought, her heart pounding. Then, an exciting idea occurred to her. The rumours that *The*

Nutcracker casting was about to be announced had been circulating for days. So many small but important roles were in it. Could Petrov possibly want to see her about one of them?

But, he asked to see Alice first, she worried, twisting her hands together. *What if it's one or the other of us?* A horrible idea was forming in Daphne's mind. Momentarily she felt ashamed that she could even be thinking it, but, deliberately hardening her heart, she heard the stockings give a slithery, sinister kind of rustle.

She sat for a while, deep in thought, then sighed, got up and went to her dressing room. "I've got a message for Alice. Have you seen her anywhere?" she asked Sophie.

"Washing her hair, I think," Sophie replied. "She's got a big dinner date. Lucky pig!" She turned and smiled at Daphne. "Françoise and I are going out for a coffee. Want to come?"

Although Daphne had had fun with the girls in the corps de ballet on many other evenings, tonight she found herself strangely reluctant to accept Sophie's friendly invitation.

She absent-mindedly touched the stockings. And the thought hit her like a tidal wave. *These girls are my RIVALS. It doesn't do to get friendly with your rivals, because*

*it's all a big competition around here. I mean, look at Alice
and me both being sent for by Petrov.*

"Sorry, can't," she said offhandedly.

Sophie shrugged and, looking in her make-up mirror,
checked to see that her lipstick was perfectly applied.
"Your loss. We're going dancing afterwards."

Daphne stared at Sophie's back for a moment, then
she said abruptly, "I'll go and give Alice her message."

The corps de ballet bathroom, with its showers and
basins, was just along the hallway. From outside the
door Daphne heard the sound of rushing water.

"Alice!" Daphne called softly. "Monsieur Petrov wants
to see you tomorrow morning at nine." There was no
reply. Daphne said the same thing again, a little bit
louder. Then she walked away. "I've told her, so that's
all right."

But if it really was all right, why did she feel so
miserable?

Next morning, Miss Tripp, at her desk outside
Petrov's door, asked sharply, "Mademoiselle Green, you
did give Alice Durocher my message?"

"Of course, Miss Tripp," Daphne assured her, the
blood rushing to her face.

The secretary pressed a button on her intercom. "I've
just confirmed that Mademoiselle Durocher did get the

message, Director General. And Mademoiselle Green is here to see you." She listened for a moment then, "You can go in," she said. Turning back to her type-writer, she tapped away. When she next looked at her watch, she was surprised to find so much time had passed. Her busy employer was certainly giving his full attention to that young woman.

The door opened and Petrov ushered Daphne out with a smile. "I have enjoyed talking to you, Miss Green," he said. Daphne flew off, wings on her heels. Monsieur Petrov had complimented her on her dancing and had asked her all about her classes with Rudolf Gorky.

"Please ask our ballet master if he can spare me a few moments at his earliest convenience," the impresario told his secretary. Within ten minutes Monsieur Philippe and Petrov were seated opposite each other in the director general's office.

"Did you tell Alice Durocher?" Philippe asked.

"I had no opportunity to tell Mademoiselle Durocher anything, because she didn't turn up," Petrov said dismissively. "You know very well I simply cannot bear, and will not reward, unreliability and unpunctuality. But Daphne Green did show up, and we have just concluded a long and fascinating talk. During the course of it, an interesting idea sprang into my mind. I'm eager to hear what you think."

"Go on," Philippe said, a smile lighting up his face.

"Our press office could generate a lot of interest with an announcement that we are giving the important role of Clara to a fourteen year old English girl in her first season at the Splendide," the impresario said. "Rudolf Gorky believes in her, as you know, but until this morning, I hadn't realised what an interesting past she has, and how well she knows Magda Magellan. There's no doubt the public will devour it all. But, the question is, can she dance the role?"

The ballet master gave a quick, definite nod, and then he grinned, impishly. "It'll set the cat among the pigeons in certain quarters. But perhaps that's no bad thing. It will, as one might say, keep everyone on their toes!"

That afternoon, the whole company assembled in the theatre for the casting announcement. Andova, displaying what she believed to be an appropriate amount of boredom, sat, filing her nails, in the second row of the stalls, a soft pink cashmere shawl draped over her shoulders.

On-stage, Monsieur Philippe consulted the sheet of paper in his hand. The company fidgeted nervously. Of course Ova would dance the Sugar Plum Fairy; the Splendide's leading man, Alexei Fedorov, would dance the Prince; and a long-time, popular Splendide member, Charles Dufond, would play Drosselmeyer, the magician. But there were many other plum roles to be assigned.

Daphne sank lower and lower in her seat as the names were called and none of them was hers. At last, in a deliberately unemotional voice, the ballet master said, "And, finally, the role of Clara will be danced by Daphne Green." There was a brief silence, then, generously, the other members of the company started to applaud. Everyone, that is, except Ova Andova. She cast Daphne a look of such hatred that it froze Daphne in her seat.

From the chaotic jumble of guilt and joy in her mind, Daphne extracted one clear thought. *Now I'm DEFINITELY changing my name.* She sat on, in a daze, waiting for the crowd around Philippe to clear and give her the chance to thank him in private.

The loud buzz of gossiping conversation stopped abruptly as, sometime later, she entered the dressing room.

"I've found out you were supposed to tell me to see Petrov this morning." Fury was written all over Alice Durocher's expressive face.

"But I did, I asked Sophie where you were and I went and told you from the other side of the door," Daphne said, her voice shrill and defensive.

Alice whirled around. "Sophie?"

"Daphne did ask me, and I did see her outside the bathroom," Sophie said, quietly.

Anguished, Alice sat down and put her head in her hands. "I must go and explain to Monsieur Petrov, but I suppose I'll never know now if he had a part in mind for me," she said miserably.

It was dusk as Daphne walked home. A little breeze ruffled all the chestnut trees on her street. But, next to Daphne, one wasn't rustling. It was shaking violently, bending almost to the ground, its branches twisted into grotesque shapes. Daphne stopped and stared. Suddenly, with no warning, she was flung backwards, as if in the grip of a hurricane. The tree exploded into a million fragments of light, a flashing spectrum of red, yellow, orange, green, blue, indigo and violet rays. Blinded, Daphne covered her eyes. She heard a voice calling her name. When she lowered her hands, Pierre Beauchamp was there, sitting on a branch. Although the arms of the tree whipped around him in the whistling gale, not a hair moved on the head of the creator of ballet.

From the eerie vacuum where she stood, Daphne watched the ordinary world going on its way. "Monsieur Beauchamp?" she gasped.

But Beauchamp didn't speak to her. Staring, with the fierce eyes of a lion into Daphne's horror-stricken ones, he only raised his finger in a grave, warning gesture.

Terrified, Daphne forced herself into stumbling flight, not daring to look behind her. Passers-by stared. One woman put out a worried hand to see if she could help. But, with unseeing eyes, Daphne brushed the hand away and ran on. Sobbing, panting, she flung herself through her front door, frantically locking it behind her.

Beauchamp had appeared so real. *But, he couldn't have been*, Daphne moaned to herself. No one else had seen him. She rocked blindly backwards and forwards on the sofa, sure she was going mad, like the girl in the *Scarlet Stockings* ballet.

The rest of the evening was a blur. She hardly moved. She didn't eat. All night, wearing every piece of warm clothing she possessed, she huddled under her blankets. She was cold, so very cold.

In the grey light of morning, she got out of bed, smiled grimly, and wrote something on a small slip of paper.

The Enchanted Riddle

Later, the postman, new on this route, stood, scratching his head, in the courtyard of the yellow house on the Rue des Arts. He read and reread the name above the letterbox of every resident. There didn't seem to be anyone living there called Daphne Green. He put each letter of his delivery into its appropriate box.

He didn't put anything into the newly-labelled box that read: D. ST. JUDE.

Chapter Twenty

The advance photographs for *The Nutcracker* went up outside the Théâtre Splendide. The biggest ones, of course, were of Ova Andova and Alexei Fedorov, but Daphne had a beautiful one of her own, captioned:

And Daphne St. Jude as Clara.

She would have been in a continual state of bliss if it hadn't been for Andova. The *assoluta* refused to recognise Daphne's new status and, scornfully, never called her anything but "Green". She sneered at Daphne's dancing, interrupted her questions to Monsieur Philippe with questions of her own, and demanded extra rehearsal time that cut into Daphne's. It got even worse when the company moved out of the rehearsal rooms and into the theatre for technical dress rehearsals.

'Techs,' as they were called, were always a nightmare that stretched the dancers to breaking point. After weeks spent blocking out and rehearsing the movements on a level floor, with piano accompaniment, the company now had to adjust to dancing on the actual ramps and staircases of the set, with a full orchestra. For the first time, Daphne was experiencing the constant, nerve-racking stops and starts as Monsieur Philippe restaged variations she'd toiled over for weeks because they didn't work on the set, or because he had to consult with the set or lighting designer, or because the wardrobe mistress came running in with a just-finished piece of costume, or because the dancers and the musicians weren't together.

The Nutcracker's techs were made even more hellish by Andova. After almost every passage she danced, she held up her hand imperiously for the orchestra to stop, then came downstage and, shading her eyes against the stage lights, called out into the auditorium, "Would it not be better if I am moving three steps forward, like *this*?," as if the whole production revolved solely around her. It was obvious that what she was really doing was showing them all that, whereas Daphne might be a rising star, it was Ova the audience was paying to see, Ova who was the prima ballerina *assoluta* of the Ballet Splendide.

Petrov, seated next to Philippe in the stalls, gritted his teeth. "This is becoming altogether too tedious. The woman is a positive menace." Rising, he called diplomatically, "Ova, my dear, you are giving a superb performance, you are completely perfect as you are. Now we must continue."

To Andova's complete satisfaction, her tactics, coupled with exhaustion and tension, were causing Daphne's dancing to deteriorate. "Petrov will see what a great mistake he has made in giving the part of Clara to an inexperienced girl of such small dancing talent!" she sniggered to Grushka.

Each night now, Daphne fell into a heavy, dreamless sleep, waking to face another day of classes, followed by a tech dragging on late into the night. "Will this never end?" she asked Alexei Fedorov. He grinned understandingly.

"I love it though, Alexei, more than anything in life."

Their duet was interrupted yet again, this time by a spotlight crisis.

Unknown to Daphne, a crisis of a different kind was brewing in Hoxton.

"It's stamped NOT KNOWN AT THIS ADDRESS," Dolly said, worriedly.

Lofty picked up the crumpled envelope. "And it's taken weeks to get back here."

"There's something horribly fishy about this, I'm afraid." Joe rose and paced up and down Dolly's kitchen.

"We haven't heard a peep out of her for months, and now this."

"I got one postcard." Dolly said. "But that was ages ago and it only had two sentences on it."

Lofty frowned. "She hasn't written to me at all."

"Ma and Pa are so worried, they even used the Cheadles' telephone last weekend to call the Splendide," Joe said, frowning. "They had to leave a message at the stage door, and Daphne still hasn't phoned them back. I don't want them to be more scared than they already are, so I'm not going to say anything to them about this letter." There was a worried silence, then Joe asked, "Do you remember how much is in our Best Of Friends post office savings account, Doll?"

"There should be quite a bit. We haven't drawn much out since Daphne went away," Dolly told him.

"We'd better go to Paris," Joe said, grimly.

As it turned out, there wasn't enough money in the post office account to pay for three people's fares and a Paris hotel, so they had to agree Lofty should let Dr. Spires in on the plan and ask for his help. Anxiously, Lofty waited outside the door of his father's Surgery, and when the last patient of the day left, he went in.

Dr. Spires listened sombrely. Then, "Of course, you can have the money," he said. "But the three of you must act responsibly. If you find out Daphne is no longer at the theatre, you must inform the French police immediately and send me a telegram. Mr. and Mrs. Green will have to be told."

"I hope it doesn't come to that, Dad," Lofty promised, his heart sinking.

The next day it was a subdued trio of Friends who boarded the train at Victoria Station. After a rough, unpleasant Channel crossing, and a train journey that seemed endless, they reached Paris's busy Gare du Nord station. Lofty had been to Paris with his parents once before, so he knew the quickest way to get around was by underground train. "I'll find out where the nearest entrance is. I've rehearsed it in French," he said. "Oú est le Métro, si'l vous plaît?" he asked a porter. The man kindly walked with them outside into the cold December night, and pointed down the street. Huddled into their winter coats, they hurried down the steps under the Métro station's illuminated entrance arch.

Joe, ever the proud Londoner, said, "We had electric trains underground twenty years before they had 'em here in France."

"Our stations haven't got marble walls and chandeliers, though," Lofty said, grinning. "So you can stop waving your Union Jack now!"

Efficiently Dolly studied a map of the train system. "This must be it." She pointed. "Place Splendide. It's in the right part of Paris."

"Not bad!" Joe admitted, as, half an hour later, they got off the sleek train and surfaced into the imposing Plaza. Opposite them shone the vast glittering, lighted theatre. Dodging traffic, they ran across the road to it.

"No wonder my letter came back," Dolly said, gazing at Daphne's photograph.

"What's this 'Daphne St. Jude' business?" Joe said angrily. "Isn't 'Green' good enough for her these days?"

"But at least we know she's all right," Lofty said. "That's what matters. And, clever girl, she's got a starring part already!"

"That's no reason not to bother writing to anyone, or letting us know she's changed her name," Dolly fumed.

There was a queue at the box office buying tickets for the evening's performance. Excited children hopped up and down by their parents' side.

"I don't think we should distract her before the show," Lofty said. "Let's see if they've got any tickets left."

"DISTRACT her! I'm going to SHAKE her when I see her. What on earth does she think she's been playing at? Ma's been so worried she's been crying her eyes out," Joe exploded.

Lofty came back after a while. "Tonight's actually the premiere. All I could get was standing room at the back."

"That suits me. We'll get out and around to the stage door faster at the end," Joe replied, grimly.

Inside the Splendide, corps de ballet dressing room no. 2 was in hot, noisy turmoil. As the dancers finished their make-up, a team of dressers worked quickly, lacing the backs of costumes and helping to adjust wigs. Above all the chaos, high up, near the ceiling, a narrow old window serenely framed the star-sprinkled December sky.

Through the loudspeakers mounted on the dressing room walls, the sound of the festive audience settling into its seats drifted in from the auditorium. There was a coughing, tapping sound, then the voice of the stage manager announced, "Ten minutes to curtain. Ladies and gentlemen of the Prologue and Beginners, to the wings, please."

There was a chorus of "Good luck, everyone!" and, with a clatter, all the dancers except Daphne were gone, banging the door behind them.

In the ringing silence, Daphne shivered with nerves. The other dressing tables were loaded with good-luck bouquets and telegrams. The only flower in front of her mirror was the single red rose Petrov had sent to all the members of the corps de ballet. She picked it up and stroked the velvety petals.

For reassurance she touched the stockings. They were as icily cold as her own hands, but after a moment, thankfully, she felt her nausea retreat. In its place came a rush of elation and excitement so powerful it made her tremble.

She took a breath and went deeply inside herself to a place where Daphne disappeared and there was only Clara. Absorbed, she didn't hear the soft click coming from the dressing room's door.

Loud applause bursting from the wall speaker brought her back to a consciousness of where she was. Daphne realised the conductor must have entered to take his bow before the performance began. Quickly, she got up to go to the wings and approached the door. She turned the door handle and pulled. Nothing happened. She pulled again, harder, and rattled the knob.

"HELP, someone, HELP me!" she yelled, her voice shaking.

Outside, in the deserted passageway, Grushka gave a satisfied smile as she pocketed the dressing room key. "I hope you will be enjoying the ballet!" she muttered meanly, slinking away.

Daphne wrenched at the door again. But, it was no good. She was locked in.

Chapter Twenty One

The overture's first happy notes filled the dressing room. Daphne's entrance, as the young girl, Clara, at her parents' Christmas party, followed a short prologue.

Don't panic, think, she told herself, her heart in her mouth. Breathing deeply, she tried to work out exactly how much time she had. She knew every step of *The Nutcracker* now, everyone else's as well as her own. *I've got about seven minutes,* she calculated. Looking wildly around the dressing room, she realised that there was only one possible means of escape. It was the narrow window, up near the ceiling.

The stockings! They'll help me to leap high enough to reach the window. She spared a second silently to thank the Splendide's architect, who had placed a ledge running all the way around the room, just below window height.

A minute had already gone by. She raced to the end of the long room. Then, running, gathering all the speed she could, she flung herself into the air. With a thankful sob, she managed to clutch onto the ledge with one hand. Her body dangling awkwardly, she grabbed the window's catch and tried with all her strength to move it. With a sickening lurch she realised the catch was so old it must have rusted shut.

Behind her, the carefree music played on.

Five minutes. She dropped back to the floor. Desperately, she scanned the dressing room's make-up tables. "Thank goodness," she breathed when she saw someone's manicure set. Grabbing its small scissors, she flung herself into another desperate grand jeté. She chopped in panic with her free hand at the rust on the catch and thought she'd got it all. But by then her arms hurt so much, she had to let go again.

Four minutes. Her third leap took her up to the window again. Now sweat was pouring off her. The catch grudgingly gave way. With a shove, she opened the window as far as it would go. But would there be enough space for her to squeeze through? "OUCH!" She landed once more on the dressing room floor, her ankle at an awkward angle. She massaged it, wincing. It didn't seem to be sprained. But she had to spend valuable seconds walking off the pain.

Three minutes. Time was running out now. With the

blood roaring in her ears, Daphne ran and leaped, both hands clutching the ledge. Twisting slowly, painfully, she pulled her slender body up and through the narrow opening. From behind her, she heard the music for her entrance scene begin.

Two minutes. She landed in the alley outside the stage door. In a flash she was through it and hurtling to the wings. She just had time to register the furious, surprised face of Andova, and then the disappointed one of her own understudy. She wrenched her mind away from the last few minutes. All that was for later.

She willed herself to think of nothing but the music. Tonight, *she* was the one fulfilling the eternal dream of Pierre Beauchamp, a human instrument expressing the most beautiful movements ever devised. Forgotten were the weeks and weeks of demanding rehearsals, the bruised and bleeding feet, the deadening exhaustion. **MADEMOISELLE ST. JUDE BLAZED ACROSS THE STAGE LIKE THE CHRISTMAS STAR**, an important critic would later write. Vaguely, she was aware of murmurs and applause. As she was aware in a different, horrible way of Andova subtly shoving her when they met on-stage, trying to make the audience believe Daphne had stumbled. But Daphne remained steady. Nothing could dim her radiance and grace.

At the end, the biggest applause of the night was, as expected, for Andova. But when Daphne stepped forward to take her curtsy, a roar of interest and approval exploded from the audience, and kept her curtseying centre stage over and over again until they let her step back into line.

Ecstatic, Daphne flashed a glance at Andova, and was appalled when she caught the *assoluta*'s mask of graciousness slipping momentarily to reveal the boiling, jealous rage beneath it. With a shudder of pure fear, Daphne realised, *she REALLY hates me now.*

As the curtain fell, and the delighted company exited into the wings, Petrov motioned to Daphne to wait. After kissing Ova on both cheeks and escorting her off the stage, the impresario returned and took both of Daphne's hands in his with fatherly pride.

"I have watched you putting your whole soul, your whole being, all the exquisite joy you find in dancing into your work," he said softly. "We like to encourage young talent at the Splendide. You have repaid in full the confidence that Monsieur Philippe and I placed in you. Go now and change. We shall celebrate later, at our party at Maxim's restaurant."

Daphne's heart overflowed. Never again could anyone possibly call her insignificant. Never again would she think of herself that way. Saying a final goodbye to the 'orphan-Daphne-who-had-been' she didn't notice the three familiar figures waiting for her among the crowd in the stage door corridor.

"DAPHNE!" Joe's loud call spun her around. She turned, slowly taking in Joe, Dolly, and Lofty holding their programmes. She took an excited step towards them but, before she could say a word, as he'd threatened to, Joe did, in fact, stride up and shake her.

"WHY HAVEN'T YOU ANSWERED OUR LETTERS?" he roared at her. "No one's heard from you for months. Ma and Pa have been making all sorts of excuses for you, but they've been beside themselves. Too busy to think of anyone but yourself, Miss Bighead? And who the hell is *Daphne St. Jude?*"

Pulling herself free, Daphne saw Dolly glowering at her. Lofty was the only one of them who didn't look as if he'd like to hit her. Weren't *any* of them going to congratulate her? The stockings felt like a sheet of ice.

"It's *my* name now," she said coldly. "I don't know if you happened to notice, but I had six curtain calls tonight. I'm not the same Daphne I was before."

At that, it was Dolly's turn to shout at her. "So that means you can do whatever you want and scare everyone to death. I suppose you can't be bothered with Hoxton or anyone in it now you're so important, Mademoiselle *St. Jude.*"

"Goodness, Dolly," Daphne replied, forcing amused disdain into her voice. "Could that be jealousy turning you so green?" With mean satisfaction, she watched Dolly's face flame at the outrageous accusation.

"I'm ashamed of you," Joe said furiously. "If you don't care about any of us, you might spare a thought for Ma and Pa. Why didn't you telephone them back? And when are you intending to come home to see them?"

Daphne shrugged affectedly. "When my Management here says I can be spared, I suppose," she said carelessly. "And I don't have any idea when that will be. The season's in progress, and it may not be for months."

"Not changed yet, my dear?" Petrov said, smiling as he passed by in his sleek fur-collared overcoat. "You're going to be late for our celebration at Maxim's."

When she was sure he couldn't hear her, Daphne called out after him, "I'm coming, Serge." None of the dancers except Andova and Alexei Fedorov addressed the dignified impresario by his first name. But Joe and Dolly and Lofty didn't know that. Daphne hoped they were suitably impressed. Shrugging, she said coolly, "I suppose I shouldn't have expected any of you to be pleased for me. Anyway, I can't talk now, I'm late for our party."

Turning on her heel, she walked quickly away.

Joe stared after her. "She said that as if she hated us," he said, miserably.

"We didn't even get a chance to tell her how good she was, and how pleased we were to see her," Lofty said, shaken.

But Dolly, being Dolly, wasn't miserable or shaken. She was straightforwardly furious. "I'll never speak to her again," she said.

Chapter Twenty Two

Daphne had told the Friends she was different now. And from the moment she turned her back on them she was. Different in her heart and different in her thoughts.

In the early hours of the morning, she sat on the floor of her apartment, her weary feet and legs raised on the arm of a chair. The emotions of the evening had stripped her nerves bare. Her terror when she believed she wouldn't get out of the dressing room. The ecstatic happiness of feeling her heart, her body, and her mind illuminated and united as she danced. The proud delight of her curtain calls. The wonder of walking down the curved staircase into the mirrored glory of Maxim's, and seeing the whole room rising to its feet to applaud her. And most of all, the appalling scene at the stage door.

The scarlet stockings felt as heavy as lead as she wearily undressed.

Next morning, in the Splendide's auditorium, Daphne

waited with the rest of the company to hear Monsieur Philippe's notes on last night's performance. Andova squirmed visibly when she heard how few criticisms he had for Daphne.

The *assoluta*'s jealousy had by now become an obsession. It got worse when the reviews for *The Nutcracker* came out. Not only was Daphne likened to the Christmas star, but the most influential newspaper critic of all had raved that, in his memory, Daphne was the most exciting new talent ever to emerge at the Ballet Splendide.

Petrov told Miss Tripp to send up Monsieur Philippe, together with the Ballet's financial director, and the chief of publicity. Of course, they'd all say it was impossible, he thought, pacing impatiently around his office.

When everyone was assembled, Petrov faced his colleagues. "I propose to you today something completely unheard of at the Splendide," he said, his deep voice rising enthusiastically. "I propose that we change the last ballet of our season." The publicity chief, whose department had already sent out subscription brochures and printed advance advertising, rose to his feet in protest, but the impresario waved him aside. "You've all read the *Nutcracker* reviews. They're screaming to see more of Andova and St. Jude dancing together. Think of what would happen if we announced a completely new ballet, one created especially for the two of them! Not only would it fill our house here in Paris, but imagine the touring possibilities. New York, London, Rome. It could make enough money to keep us afloat for years to come."

There was a short impressed silence at the impresario's daring and imagination. Monsieur Philippe was the first to break it. "But, my dear Petrov," he said "How could we possibly do it in so short a time?"

"I know, I *know*," Petrov said. "That's why we must start this minute. I already have two or three possible scenarios on my desk. Miss Tripp will make sure you each have a copy of them by lunchtime." Shrewdly, he turned to Philippe. "I shall announce this to the company this afternoon. We can expect that not everyone will be pleased to hear they won't be dancing the roles they thought they would be. We must do what we can to preserve calm."

The buzz of rumour and speculation died away as Petrov, with Philippe by his side, came on-stage. In total silence the impresario made his announcement. Then he left the stage briskly, before any questions — to which he didn't yet have answers — could be asked. The ballet master stayed behind to deal with all the incredulous reactions. Amid the turmoil, Daphne slipped out and ran like someone possessed to her dressing room.

Within minutes, Miss Tripp buzzed the intercom switch on her telephone. "Monsieur Petrov," she announced," "Mademoiselle St. Jude is here to see you."

"Hmm, *The Scarlet Stockings*. An intriguing title," Petrov said a few moments later, turning the pages of the script, which Daphne, panting, had handed him. "And how did you acquire this piece of work?"

"It was stuffed away backstage at an old theatre in London. It had dust all over it, so it must have been there for ages."

Examining the paper, spotted with age, and the old-fashioned printing, Petrov drummed his fingers on his desk and mused, "No payments to the author, then. Very attractive."

"And look at the back," Daphne urged. "Everything's there — all the music and the sketches for the sets and costumes."

"Even more attractive, my dear, given how little time we have to pull this off. Very well, I shall begin to read this instant."

Daphne only had to wait until the next morning to find out the impresario had been as good as his word.

Summoned by Miss Tripp, she was warmly greeted by Petrov and Philippe. "We have examined your scenario and we are in agreement. *The Scarlet Stockings* will make a great impact. We wish you to be the first to know that Bronislava Nijinska has agreed to come to Paris to choreograph it," Petrov said.

"Nijinska!" Daphne exclaimed. How had he pulled that off so quickly? He must have been working all night. Nijinska was the brilliantly talented Russian ballerina and choreographer, and sister of Nijinsky, the most famous male dancer in the world.

Smiling understandingly at Daphne perched on the very edge of her chair, Petrov quickly added, "You, of course, will dance the part of the owner of the scarlet stockings. Madame Andova will dance the other important role, the Pursuer." Rising, Daphne impulsively threw her arms around the impresario's neck, her words of thanks buried in the shoulder of his beautifully cut grey flannel suit.

Patting her shoulder, Petrov said, "Monsieur Philippe and I have decided to give Alice Durocher her own solo, an opportunity for her to shine, but please say nothing of all this until after I announce it this afternoon. First, I must speak to our prima ballerina *assoluta*."

★ ★ ★

What happened in Andova's dressing room became first-class gossip material at the Splendide for weeks.

"NO, NO, NO!" Ova yelled, her face purple with fury. "From what you have told me of this part, my face will not even be seen. I shall be wearing a hideous mask. I am not even entering until Act Two."

Petrov tried to calm her down. "It is a great, showy role. Only a truly great dancer could carry it off," he urged. "Your reviews will all applaud your courage, your acting, your strength."

But Ova wasn't having any of it. She picked up a crystal bottle of Ova and flung it against the wall, where it splintered with a resounding crash, flooding the dressing room and the whole corridor outside it with the smell of bluebells.

What a mess, Grushka thought angrily. *And I am the one who will be having to clean it up!*

In the corps de ballet dressing room, a stagehand appeared. He had come to move all Daphne's possessions. Petrov was giving her a dressing room of her own.

The dancers clustered around her. "Is it true?" Sophie asked. "We've heard Andova's been cast as some sort of a raving demon!" Amazed, yet again, by the speed and accuracy of the Splendide's rumour mill, all Daphne could answer was, "I'm sorry, all of you , I'm not allowed to say anything until Monsieur Petrov does."

"Stuck up cow!" she heard someone say, as she followed her possessions out of the room. Daphne shrugged. The corps de ballet. Always jealous and small-minded. Why should she care what they thought about her now?

Rehearsals for *The Scarlet Stockings* began. To the utter astonishment of all at the Splendide, from Petrov on down, Andova behaved perfectly. She was charming to her countrywoman, Nijinska, and astoundingly, worry-ingly pleasant to Daphne. Rehearsals were filled with enthusiasm and cooperation. Madame Nijinska was an inspiring choreographer. A ballerina herself, she knew the value of allowing the dancers to participate in the creation of their roles. With almost magical speed, the choreography was coming to life.

Every single day, now that she was dancing the heroine of his *Scarlet Stockings* into being, Daphne hoped for a message from Pierre Beauchamp. She had prepared herself to be scared to death again if he suddenly appeared. But he didn't. Not even in her dreams. Bitterly disappointed, Daphne drove herself even harder to reach her goal of perfection.

At rehearsal Daphne marvelled at how nice Ova was being to her. But, if she'd known the *assoluta*'s true feelings, she would have been very frightened indeed.

"Unbearable, the arrogance, the condescension of this one. She should have been put in her place the last time. I am still not understanding what went wrong."

"Very strange," Grushka rumbled in agreement. While *The Nutcracker* company had been on-stage, she'd returned and unlocked the door, leaving the key in it. After examination, the near disaster had been put down to the lock's age and use, and it had been immediately replaced.

But, now, even the stolid Grushka was alarmed. She'd never seen her employer in such a state. "My Ovushka," she pleaded. "Please, you are making yourself ill."

"Pah!" was Ova's only reply.

By April, the company was in techs. Presenting himself one morning in Petrov's office, Philippe said nervously, "Serge, I am afraid. Things are going too smoothly!"

Petrov laughed. "We have prepared carefully. Of course everything is going smoothly. Don't be such a dreadful old pessimist, my friend!"

The final tech before opening night was such a complete disaster that the ballet master had to remind himself of the old theatrical saying, 'A bad dress rehearsal means a great performance.' As he watched, distraught, he prayed that it would hold true.

Worn out and edgy, the company dragged itself through the second act. Daphne whirled across the stage, her mane of artfully tangled 'mad' hair, streaming round her shoulders. Andova, with a brilliantly accomplished triple mid-air spin, exultantly followed her to the brink of the abyss.

Then it happened.

Under the open trapdoor, the padded platform, there to catch Daphne as she fell, jammed. From under the stage, the booming voice of the chief stagehand bellowed "STOP!"

The rehearsal came to an unhappy halt while a team of stagehands down below checked the apparatus's network of ropes. As the minutes passed, Petrov, tapping his foot in his seat in the auditorium, consulted his watch. It was obvious the breakdown was a major one that would take time to repair. After a quick consultation with Nijinska he dismissed the company and orchestra for the night.

But Ova did not return to her dressing room like everyone else. Stealthily, she darted down the dark staircase leading under the stage. In the distance, in front of her of her, three stagehands clustered around the trapdoor platform. The *assoluta* slunk back into the shadows. After a few moments, she let out a hiss of relief as one of them, little more than a boy, left the huddled group.

Groping on a distant shelf for a pair of pliers, the young stagehand, Robert, got the fright of his life when, out of nowhere, Andova suddenly grabbed his arm.

"I have a special task for you to perform tomorrow when we open," she murmured, her violet eyes blazing. "You *will* be doing this special task, because if you are not doing it I will *make sure* you will no longer have work as a stagehand anywhere. You are believing I can do this, *yes?*"

The terrified young man trembled. The power and influence of Madame Andova were legendary. He was new at the Splendide. He had recently married. Only today, he'd learned his wife was pregnant. Speechlessly, he nodded.

"Then you will be here at the interval. I will be telling you then what you must be doing."

With a final threatening glare, the prima ballerina *assoluta* melted back into the absolute darkness.

Chapter Twenty Three

The romantic, chiselled features of her leading man appeared around Daphne's dressing room door. "Good luck tonight, my little English swanling!" Fedorov said, kissing his hand to her and sweeping back his mane of silver blond hair. "Let us hope all our reviews are raves!" Then he was gone. The sounds of the orchestra tuning up filtered into the room as Daphne nervously bent to drink in the perfume of the vast arrangement of scarlet roses Petrov had sent her for *this* opening night.

"Your bodice, Mademoiselle St. Jude." The shy voice of her young dresser, Clarice, interrupted Daphne's far-ranging thoughts. For a brief moment, she'd been thinking longingly of other sorts of flowers, home-grown ones — peonies, dahlias and old roses. Flowers that she'd once helped to sell from a market stall.

I mustn't think about that tonight, she told herself. Petrov had hinted of raising her status to prima ballerina if she made a great success of *The Scarlet Stockings*. Once she became a star, what would it matter what the Friends had or hadn't said when they got back to Hoxton?

The loving, reproachful faces of Carlo and Maria materialised and floated in front of her closed eyes.

Daphne cowered back in her chair, her hands to her face.

GO AWAY, I DON'T WANT YOU HERE, she shrieked to herself. With guilty hands she reached down to touch the stockings.

Instantly, she felt her mind clear and find its cold balance again.

Straightening her shoulders she got up from her dressing table. For some extraordinary reason she wasn't nervous any more. It was as if this night was what she had been destined for all her life.

Clarice laced up the scarlet bodice, with its deep slashes of orange satin, and helped Daphne into her floating scarlet skirt. "Mademoiselle looks beautiful," she said, her face glowing with admiration.

Daphne bent to tie her ballet shoes, then sat quietly, her head bowed. Her legs shimmered with electric energy. The magic had worked. Tonight, her painfully hard work would be rewarded. Tonight, her destiny would unfold.

In the wings Daphne saw Andova waiting to watch Act I. Her demonic costume was hidden under a silk dressing gown. Grushka stood next to her, the Pursuer's menacing sculpted mask in her hands. Daphne was relieved when the *assoluta* gave her a gracious nod. She wanted nothing ugly, such as jealousy, to touch her this evening.

"Daphne!" a soft voice said at her shoulder. Alice Durocher stood there in costume. Reaching out her hand she said generously, "Good luck, tonight. You deserve it."

But Daphne turned her back, ignoring Alice as if she hadn't spoken. Crushed, the other young dancer walked away. Alice fumed. St. Jude was the nastiest, meanest person she'd ever met. She was even *worse* than Madame Andova. At least *she* never pretended to be anyone's friend.

Oblivious to what had just happened, Daphne's mind focused itself to a pinpoint of diamond-bright concentration. Nijinska's daring choreography was ingrained in her from so much rehearsal. She knew her body would move automatically. But it was her soul she was calling on now, summoning it to express the overwhelming gratitude she felt for the gift of the scarlet stockings and for the joy of fulfilment they'd brought into her life. Adrenaline coursed through her as she rose on pointe. She drifted exquisitely onto the stage and into her part of a young, innocent ballerina about to discover the power of magic.

Act I concluded with the heroine's sensational leap off into the wings, a mirror of the enchanted night when Daphne had made her own discovery in Hoxton's market square. The curtains swept closed, then a spotlight came up to illuminate their central fold. Daphne stepped shyly through into the dazzling light. As one, the audience rose to its feet, the applause and cheers rising to the Splendide's magnificent ceiling, then dropping back into the huge auditorium to drench it in shattering sound. For more than five minutes the ovation went on. The floor around Daphne's feet was covered so thickly with flowers tossed by the audience, that it would take two stagehands the rest of the intermission to clear it.

At last the cheering crowd let her go. Daphne flew to her dressing room for the complete make-up and costume change that would turn her from an innocent girl into a selfish, sophisticated *assoluta*.

In the farthest corner below the stage, Robert pleaded and protested. But, through its malevolent mask, the familiar voice replied, "Pah, it is nothing, a little joke only. I have made arrangements. All is being quite safe. Now GO."

The applause for Daphne and Ova grew and grew

throughout the second act. At last, trapped on a crag high above the stage, Daphne danced her terror as the audience sat in tense silence. The music crashed out as her Pursuer leaped onto the jutting space behind her. Above their heads, the midnight sky was pierced over and over again by lurid flashes of lightning and deafening cracks of thunder.

With passionate intensity, Daphne flung herself from the crag in Nijinska's sensational climax. The audience held its breath, as she seemed almost to hover in mid-air before, with one last despairing gesture, she plummeted into the abyss.

As the final tragic chords crashed out and the Pursuer stood high above the stage, arms raised in triumph, the young stagehand did what he had been ordered to do. He pulled a lever. The waiting platform fell away, taking Daphne with it into the dark.

Falling, falling, Daphne thought despairingly of Beauchamp's solemn warning about the deadly power of the scarlet stockings. *Choosing, you will test me*, tolled inside her head like a graveyard bell. *I've chosen death*, she thought in terror as the ground rushed up to receive her.

Seconds later, her scarlet figure lay twisted on the Théâtre Splendide's stone-flagged floor.

Chapter Twenty Four

The entire audience stood applauding wildly as the curtains slowly closed. But after several minutes, when it was obvious they were not going to open again, the cheers died away, leaving behind them an uncomfortable, puzzled silence. At last, the centre of the curtain moved, but instead of Daphne, it was Monsieur Philippe who emerged and stood, spot-lit, at the front of the stage. Before he even began speaking, a crescendo of speculation began. He raised his hand, and the theatre fell into ghastly silence.

"Ladies and gentlemen, there will be no curtain call tonight," the ballet master said, his voice trembling. "Regrettably, Mademoiselle St. Jude has become ill."

The clamour of appalled reaction could be heard clearly through the still-open trapdoor as the Ballet Splendide's doctor leant over Daphne's unconscious figure. "There is a faint heartbeat," he told Petrov, who, for the first time ever in public, had lost his unshakeable calm and was running his fingers distractedly through his hair. "We must immediately summon an ambulance," the doctor continued urgently. "No one must touch her until it comes. Only the hospital can tell us if there are serious internal injuries."

Serge motioned a shaken Miss Tripp forward. "See to it, Eunice," he said.

Hurrying away, Miss Tripp thought he must be in shock. He had never called her Eunice before.

"Tell Daphne's dresser to come with blankets. Also, tell the publicity chief I need him immediately in my office," Petrov called after her.

On-stage, clustered together in frightened, puzzled groups, the dancers awaited their impresario. Ova stood silently apart. Tight-lipped, Petrov entered from the wings. "There has been an accident of such gravity I hardly know how to speak of it," he said, sombrely. "Mademoiselle St. Jude is alive, but in grave condition. An investigation will begin immediately to find out how this tragedy could possibly have occurred."

Petrov held up his hand to silence the outcry that met his announcement. "Mademoiselle de la Faisanderie," he said, his eyes searching Sophie out, "I believe you were Mademoiselle St. Jude's neighbour in

225

her former dressing room. Would you be kind enough to present yourself in my office. I must ask for your help."

From off-stage, Miss Tripp beckoned. "They are coming at once from the Hôpital St. Suplice."

The Splendide's whole company and staff stood in silence as Daphne's blanket-covered body, still unconscious, was carried out to the waiting ambulance. Among the watchers was the stagehand, Robert, shame and shock written vividly all over his face.

By the time Petrov reached his office, Philippe, Madame Nijinska, the Splendide's studious-looking, bespectacled publicity chief and Sophie were waiting for him. "Mademoiselle de la Faisanderie, have you any idea of where in London we might find Daphne's family? As you can imagine, it is imperative they be informed at once." Petrov said.

"I haven't heard her speak of them for months," Sophie replied, trembling. "But I believe they are called Carlo and Maria Green, and that they live in a part of London called Hoxton. Daphne did once say they're not on the telephone, although their neighbours are, and that's how she told her family about her success at the audition." Her face fell. "Wait, let me try to remember that name." She thought intently. "Oh thank goodness, I do remember. It was Harry and Sheila Cheadle."

"We are very grateful to you, mademoiselle," Petrov told her. "You may go and rejoin your colleagues now." Sadly, Sophie left the room.Buzzing Miss Tripp, the impresario said, "Be good enough to contact the London telephone operator and ask her to get us Mr. and Mrs. Harry Cheadle in the Hoxton district of London." He turned to the others. "This is a disaster of enormous proportions."

Miss Tripp knocked. "I'm sorry to interrupt, Monsieur le Director General, but there's a young stagehand outside insisting he must see you urgently. He says he has information regarding tonight's tragedy."

"Send him in immediately." Scowling, Petrov said, "I am very much afraid we are not going to like what he has to tell us. I have my own suspicions. I pray they are wrong."

Robert entered, his face drained of all colour. Petrov motioned the scared young man brusquely to a chair and waited in stony silence.

"She said she had made arrangements, that I must keep quiet, it was only a little joke and nothing would happen. I didn't trust it, but I forced myself to believe her." The words tumbled out of Robert in an agonised burst. "She swore if I didn't do what she said, I would be dismissed immediately from the Splendide and she would ensure I found no other work."

There was a shocked silence. There was no need to ask who *she* was. Piteously, Robert continued, "I will never cease blaming myself for my part in this. I would never have done it except I was terribly afraid of Madame Andova. You see I have a young wife and a baby on the way. I have come to you to ask if Mademoiselle St. Jude dies, must I go to church and confess to murder? It is a question I cannot ask my wife or my parents, for they will not judge my actions as I know they should be judged." He broke down, his hands over his face.

The air in Petrov's office seemed to vibrate with tension. Then: "Young man," the impresario said sternly, "you will take a month off, without pay. And, during this month, you will tell absolutely no one, not even your wife, of what has occurred. Your conscience must bear the appalling weight of this guilt on its own. If, at the end of the month, you have kept silent, you will recover your position with us."

Robert nodded gratefully, then with a final, whispered, "Please believe how sorry I am," he fled.

"I must say I pity that boy," Philippe exclaimed as

the door closed behind Robert. "Of course he should have immediately reported his conversation, but we've all seen Andova's ability to force her will on others. I can't say I'm surprised that his conscience was no match for her insane ego and malice. She cannot stay here, Serge. She cannot ever set foot on our stage again."

"Leave that to me," Petrov said, his voice like ice. "I will deal with Madame Andova."

Miss Tripp knocked again. "Edouard is here. He says there's a crowd of reporters at the stage door."

The publicity chief jumped to his feet. "I'll go at once, Director General, and explain it was a tragic accident that we are now looking into. I think I can hold them at bay, although they'll certainly go off to make a nuisance of themselves at the hospital." He went out at a run.

"Whisky?" Petrov asked Nijinska and Philippe, picking up a cut-glass decanter. "I shall go and see Andova immediately after the London call comes through. Immediately, that is, after I have a glass of this." His hand trembled as he poured out three glasses. The intercom buzzed.

"We have Madame Cheadle on the line."

Petrov spoke as calmly as possible in explanation, but even so, Sheila's cry of shock was so loud everyone in the room heard it. "Would you be kind enough to inform Monsieur and Madame Green of their daughter's whereabouts in the St. Suplice Hospital," Petrov said. He waited while a shocked gabble came from the phone, then interrupted the flow. "The Ballet Splendide will, of course, pay for them to come immediately to Paris. My secretary, Miss Tripp, will arrange everything. Unfortunately, it is too late for Monsieur and Madame to travel tonight. But I will expect them here tomorrow. My driver will meet their train and take them straight to the hospital. Please assure Monsieur and Madame Green that Daphne is in the thoughts and prayers of all of us here. Thank you, Madame Cheadle. Goodbye."

Petrov drained his glass in four deep gulps. He shuddered. "Now for Andova," he said grimly.

"Would you like me to come with you?" Philippe offered.

"I think it best that no one but Andova and myself hear this conversation," the impresario replied.

It was deserted backstage. Everyone had gone, fleeing the echoes of tragedy sweeping through the silent theatre. But under the door of dressing room no.1 there was a line of light. Knocking, Petrov was admitted by a stone-faced Grushka. Andova lay slumped among the furs of her daybed, an ice-bag held to her head. She hadn't taken off her Pursuer costume, and from her grey face two violet eyes blazed out like lanterns. She seemed dazed.

Petrov spoke coldly. "Madame Andova, the true facts of this evening's disaster have been made known to me. I have respected you for many years, and even now I cannot believe you capable of such malice. I can only think you have suffered some kind of breakdown. As of this moment, your contract as prima ballerina *assoluta* of the Ballet Splendide is terminated. However, because of our years of collaboration, I have decided to protect your reputation. We are announcing that the shock of tonight's experience has caused you to cancel the remaining performances of the season. Naturally, we will be withdrawing *The Scarlet Stockings* from our programme."

At last Ova spoke. Reaching out a trembling hand, she pleaded, "It was not I who did this, Serge. It was the hand of fate."

"You are deluded, Madame Andova," Petrov replied with disgust. "Be extremely careful what you say about this matter. If the truth were ever to emerge it would fill the front pages for months, and you would face prosecution. Every triumph of your brilliant career would turn to ashes and your name would signify shame for all time." He turned on his heel and left the room.

Grushka took her shuddering childhood charge in her arms. "Never mind, Ovushka," she crooned. "I will always be with you wherever we go." Staring blankly into space, Ova made no response.

Petrov sat bleakly at his desk until the hospital's senior surgeon telephoned to say that, as far as they could tell, there was no bleeding from internal injuries, although Mademoiselle St. Jude had broken both her legs. She had not yet recovered consciousness. A spine specialist had been summoned from Switzerland. "We are all in your hands, Doctor," Petrov said wearily. "I will be with you shortly, although Mademoiselle's parents are not expected from London until tomorrow afternoon."

Sorrowfully, Petrov began to work out the complicated plans necessary to keep the Splendide open and in performance now he had withdrawn *The Scarlet Stockings*. The sun was rising as he left the theatre for his home.

A few hours later, immaculate as ever, he sat in the office of the hospital's director. It had been sympathetically offered for his use, since it was just one floor away from the room where Daphne lay. Knowing the truth of what had really happened, the impresario was dreading the arrival of Carlo and Maria Green more than he had ever dreaded anything in his life before. There was a knock, and Miss Tripp stuck her head round the door. "Mr. and Mrs. Green are here. They're upstairs by the bedside." Petrov raised his eyebrows questioningly at her.

"Still unconscious, I believe," the secretary replied, shaking her head sadly.

Miserably, Petrov knocked on the door of Daphne's room and heard a muttered, "Come in." Carlo and Maria sat on either side of Daphne, each holding one of her hands. Their eyes were red. Maria took a crumpled handkerchief from her pocket. "Joe told us she was coming 'ome soon. 'Ee said she was full of life when 'ee saw 'er at Christmas."

"I am more deeply sorry about this than I can possibly express," Petrov said, quietly. "I have the greatest possible affection for your daughter. That this should have happened while she was in my care is something I will mourn my whole life."

Shakily Carlo said, "The doctor's just told us they're going to set 'er legs today. They was just waiting for us to get 'ere. But 'ee can't say whether they'll ever be strong enough for 'er to dance again."

As Petrov put his hand on Carlo's shoulder in sympathy, Carlo said sadly, "And that was the only thing she ever wanted." He turned to Maria. "At least she'll always know she was once a star with the Splendide, luv."

Pitifully, Maria held out a brown paper bag. "They've given us this," she said. "'Er costume. They 'ad to cut it off. I expect you'll want it back."

"My dear Madame Green," Petrov said sorrowfully, "I beg you, please keep it. Perhaps one day she might want to look at it again." A leaden silence fell then the impresario asked, gently, "Have you thought, yet, about your daughter's medical treatment? Our doctors in Paris are very skilled. The Ballet Splendide will, of course, be responsible for all costs incurred in her recovery."

Maria shook her head. "Carlo and me 'ave decided we'll be taking Daphne back to 'Oxton as soon as possible."

PART FOUR

'Knowing, you will challenge me.'

Chapter Twenty Five

Daphne regained consciousness. When she opened her eyes, the first thing she saw was Carlo and Maria smiling at her. For a moment, Daphne was utterly confused. Was she in Hoxton? Then she heard someone outside her door speaking French. Memory flooded sickeningly back.

"That's our gel," Carlo said, looking as if someone had just handed him the moon. "Good morning to you!"

Horrified, Daphne felt a scalding wash of red flood into her cheeks. "Mum, Dad!" she said brokenly. "I never wrote to you. I didn't invite you to my opening night. And now you've had to come all the way to Paris. I'm so, so sorry." She broke down, sobbing. Too ashamed to look into their eyes, she raised both hands and covered her face.

Watching the tears pouring through Daphne's fingers, Maria said gently, "You're all right, luv. That's the only thing wot matters. We can talk about every-thing wot's 'appened when you're feeling stronger."

Daphne gripped their hands.

After a painful few days Daphne did begin to feel a little better. At least physically. But she lay listlessly in her hospital bed. Oddly, she wasn't at all curious about how the accident had happened. "What does it matter, now? If my legs don't heal properly I won't be able to dance any more." she said despairingly to Carlo and Maria.

"That bone specialist said your spine 'adn't been damaged. 'Ee said it was a miracle seeing 'ow far you fell," Maria said, trying to cheer Daphne up. "We want you to come 'ome, luv. Would you like that, while you get better?"

"It doesn't make any difference to me where I go, Mum," Daphne said in a whisper. After that, she hardly spoke another word, except to insist she wouldn't see any of the people who came from the Ballet Splendide. "No, no, no one. You don't understand. I don't want anyone to see me like this and go away and say 'Poor Daphne, she used to be a ballerina.'"

Carlo's face creased miserably. "But, luv, your real friends won't care about that."

"If I can't spend my life doing the thing I love the most, what's the point of anything?" Daphne shouted.

"Let 'er be," Maria whispered. "It's too 'ard for 'er 'ere. Let's see what 'appens when we get 'er right away from Paris."

As soon as she'd been able to talk, Daphne had asked a nurse what had happened to her costume. "I'm afraid it was in shreds after the doctors in the emergency room finished cutting it off you," the nurse answered sympathetically. "I'm sorry."

So, with dull despair, Daphne realised that there was nothing left of the scarlet stockings. Of course, Monsieur Beauchamp had taken them away from her. She had received the sternest, most serious of warnings that they existed to follow her own will and the wishes of her heart. And she had sworn a solemn oath to remember it always and choose her behaviour accordingly.

Each time she awoke shouting and crying in the night, the nurses thought it was her injuries that were shattering her sleep. But Daphne knew it was all the people she'd betrayed — the people who'd rescued her and had faith in her — who were haunting her.

No wonder Monsieur Beauchamp took the stockings back. There must be hundreds and hundreds of dancers who deserve them more than I did, she agonised, over and over again.

Carlo and Maria couldn't bear watching her helpless weeping. Desperate measures were called for. A few days later, Daphne heard a commotion in the hallway.

Someone important's come, she thought without interest. *Probably the spine specialist again.* But it wasn't.

The door opened and a husky voice said, "Darling, this room is too, too depressing. We must get you up and about."

Daphne stared at the mink-draped, flower-laden figure in amazement. "Magda! What are you doing here?" An awestruck nurse came in, gazed at the famous face, and took the huge bunch of roses away to put them in vases.

Pulling up a chair, Magda sat down by the side of the bed. "Let me look at you, darling. Oh dear, I'm glad I came. You do look rather as if a tractor has dragged you through a farmyard backwards! Quite an amazing collection of bruises. I must remember them, they'd be awfully good if I ever switch from musical comedy to dramatic realism!"

For the first time since her opening night, Daphne smiled. "Oh, Magda you can't possibly, possibly imagine how glad I am to see you. Everyone keeps saying how lucky I am to be alive. You're the only person who could understand how I feel."

"Darling, of course I do. You're devastated. You wish you could die. There's nothing left for you."

Daphne nodded miserably. "Here," Magda said, handing her a gauzy, perfumed handkerchief. "Blow your nose. I've come to tell you you're an idiot!"

Daphne gaped at her.

"Have you forgotten what I told you when we first met?" She picked up Daphne's limp hand. "About starting at the bottom? It worked then and it's going to work now. Your legs will heal, and, one step at a time, you'll walk again. And after that, who knows? You're only fourteen, you're strong, you're healthy, you know what it means to work your body hard. You've got a will of iron. What on earth could stop you from getting completely better?" Magda Magellan was gone. It was sensible Maggie Morris from Shoreditch Daphne heard.

"Do you really think I'll be able to dance again?" Daphne asked quaveringly.

"Unless you're not the Daphne Green I know." Magda peered at Daphne's subdued face again. "It's not just dancing, is it? Any other problems our advice bureau can help you with?"

Daphne's voice was so low Magda had to put her head on the pillow to hear it. "I've been the stupidest person in the world. Someone I really respected gave me some advice and I completely ignored it. And I won't get a second chance."

"Join the club. You're looking at a leading member of the 'If I'd Only Listened' Brigade. Cheer up, ducks. At your young age it's too soon to clutch your forehead and vow to live a life of penitence and sacrifice from now on! Use your energy on yourself for now and let fate decide what She will."

Daphne smiled a watery smile. "Goodness, you're a tonic, Magda. They should patent you and sell you at every chemist's shop in the world!"

"Could I be a lovely shade of green, darling, and be in a gorgeous little bottle?"

As the day went on, gratefully, Daphne found her spirits lifting. She could even feel the stirring of a few tiny threads of energy.

"I'm in rehearsals again," Magda finally said. "Some dreary thing George talked me into. I don't suppose anyone sane will want to come and see it! I said I'd only be away for a day." Gathering her magnificent white fur coat around her, she said goodbye to Daphne, signed some autographs for the group of giggling, gazing nurses, and was gone in a wave of perfume.

Although Daphne felt flat and exhausted after the

aura of excitement that always surrounded Magda had evaporated, she forced herself to sit up and ask her nurse to hand her *How to Teach Yourself Ballet*. Maria had brought it over, at Daphne's request, from the Rue des Arts.

Perhaps it wasn't too late? She hadn't died and there were, after all, two more lines to the riddle.

Chapter Twenty Six

Joe stuck his head round Daphne's bedroom door. "There's a reporter here from the *Hoxton Gazette*, Your Famousness. He craves the favour of an interview!" Teasing Daphne about her Parisian celebrity was Joe's way of showing her she was forgiven. Accepting the bitter sting in the tail was Daphne's way of acknowledging how thoroughly she deserved it.

In hospital, and then while she was being carefully moved back to Hoxton, Daphne had pondered the riddle's next line, *Knowing, you will challenge me*. Because, even though the stockings had gone for good, she'd decided to follow the puzzle to its end. Deeply ashamed, she'd forced herself to relive her behaviour at the Splendide step-by-step. *I was so selfish, I was willing to hurt everybody and risk everything, even my life*, she'd anguished. *I know that now. It looks as though the challenge will be my choosing to stop pitying myself and trying to make up for what I did.*

Joe hovered by her bed.

"All right. I'll do the interview if the reporter doesn't ask me about the accident," Daphne told him. "I don't want to think about that. Who is it, anyway?"

"Reg Paisley, that bloke who interviewed us when we did the Flags of All Nations. He said he's been 'following your career with interest!'" Joe helped Daphne to sit up and brush her hair. "If you ask me, though," he said, laughing, "the only thing Reg really does with interest is gaze into a pint of beer!"

Daphne smiled and said hopefully, "Oh, Joe, it is good to be back in Hoxton. Perhaps if I tell Reg Paisley that, Dolly will read it and see I'm not the same stuck up beast I was in Paris."

Joe didn't say anything, because the memory of yesterday, when he and Lofty had gone to see Dolly, was only too fresh in his mind.

"Won't you at least come and see her?" Joe had pleaded.

"Yes, go on, prove that everyone with red hair hasn't got a terrible temper!" Lofty joked, taken aback by Dolly's glowering expression. "Daphne's really been through hell and it's changed her."

"It isn't a question of having a temper, you idiots," Dolly had stormed. "She broke her solemn oath to be an eternal Friend. She threw around wild accusations and cut us to our hearts. Jealous! Only someone really vain and spiteful and unfair could even think that. And then she sent us packing. That was her business. What I've chosen to do about it is mine." Dolly was adamant.

So, disappointed, that's where Joe and Lofty had been forced to leave the matter.

"Give her time," Joe now said. "You know what a stubborn old thing she is. Anyway, I'm glad you're going to talk to Reg. Ready?"

The rattly old train gave a particularly vicious bump. A crocodile-skin hatbox fell off the overhead rack and landed with a mean thump on Grushka's foot. "Son of a vodka-swilling potato farmer!" she swore.

Ova Andova's thickly mascara'd eyelashes fluttered and opened. "Where are we, Grushka?" she asked, sitting up and pulling her silver fox- fur coat around her shoulders. "Brrrrr, it is cold. Bring me tea. Put some vodka in it."

Grushka lumbered to her feet, bracing herself against the swaying of the carriage. She drew up the window blind. Flat green fields trundled by. Herds of black-and-white cows grazed peacefully. "We are nowhere, Ovushka," she grumbled. "Not a café, not a theatre am I seeing."

The Enchanted Riddle

The train creaked to yet another of its unexplained stops. The carriage door flew open to reveal a huge man with dramatic black moustaches, dressed in a red uniform with so many medals and so much gold braid he looked like a general, at least. "Welcome to Doomania!" he boomed. "Your passports, please."

Ova gaped at him unbecomingly. This man was a lowly customs official? If he wasn't a Doomanian general, what on earth, in the name of all the former tsars of Mother Russia, did they look like? She shuddered. That it should have come to this. That she, the great Madame Ova Andova, should be reduced to taking a position as prima ballerina *assoluta* in the archduchy of Doomania. What was Doomania, anyway? Just a little tin-pot country no more than eighty miles long by forty miles wide, nestled in the middle of Europe.

The Splendide's publicity chief had done his work well. And the stagehand, Robert, had kept his promise to say nothing to anyone. The actual story of how Daphne St. Jude came to fall through the stage's trapdoor had not come to light. But there'd been rumours. In a ballet company there were always rumours. And those rumours had spread. To her disgust Andova had received only one offer for her valuable services, so strangely and suddenly available.

One morning an envelope was delivered to her vulgarly opulent Paris apartment. The envelope was a striking shade of green, with an ornate gold crest embossed on it. This emblem consisted of a crowned bird that was supposed to be a peacock but looked rather more like an ostrich. The bird was perched uncomfortably on two crossed swords, underneath which were the words, **ROYAL ARCHDUCHY OF DOOMANIA**. Inside was a flattery-filled letter from the Archduchess, saying she had decided to start her own ballet company and would be honoured if Andova would consent to lead it.

"Bring me the atlas. We will see what is this Doomania," Ova had snapped. Her face had looked like thunder when she saw how tiny it was. But what was she to do? A dancer must dance. And the money offered, after all, was generous, befitting her status.

So now here she was on the Doomanian border. The train's baggage compartment was loaded to the roof with her matching monogrammed luggage and Grushka's two small, battered holdalls.

The customs officer saluted. "We are honoured by your presence, Madame Andova. I myself have seen you dance. Magnificent." He withdrew with another crisp salute.

This was more like it. Perhaps it would be tolerable

for a short time, Ova mused, sipping her vodka-laced tea. The capital city may be exciting and gay.

It wasn't.

As the train puffed into the shabby station, a welcoming band struck up a boring tune, presumably the Doomanian national anthem. An antiquated horse-drawn carriage waited to convey Ova to the Royal Palace. Its elderly footman, dressed in another improbably grand Doomanian uniform, bowed as he helped her in. Grushka he left to clamber aboard by herself.

"Pah!" Ova said disgustedly. "This capital city is more like a backward village in Russia." But when the palace appeared, it was a surprising white marvel of delicately ornate architecture, with gold turrets and spires reaching up towards the brilliantly blue sky. The carriage clattered through imposing gates, flanked by sentry boxes, and into a huge and impressive courtyard.

A distinguished personage waited at the foot of the sweeping stairs of the palace's main entrance. "What is this person?" Ova snickered to Grushka. "An admiral, I am supposing!" But it was the palace's majordomo, the chief household servant.

"Her Royal Highness, the Archduchess, awaits you in the grounds. Would you be so kind as to follow me?" He set off at a strutting trot.

They found the archduchess kicking a patch of nettles outside a rundown barn. Her fluffy blonde hair was tied up in girlish ribbons most unsuitable for a woman of her age. "Madame Andova!" she gushed, holding out both her hands. "What an honour you have done us. What a triumph we shall make together, here in Doomania."

Ova looked disdainfully around her. They seemed to be standing in some sort of farmyard. "Show me the theatre where we shall be making this triumph," she replied ungraciously.

The door of the barn opened. A herd of black-and-white cows ambled out.

"My dear, here it is. Imagine it, of course, after renovation!" the archduchess exclaimed.

Ova staggered. There was a filthy upturned bucket close by. She plopped down on it, her hand to her throat. "Grushka. Vodka," she croaked.

Chapter Twenty Seven

"Never saw plaster casts come off so easily," Doctor Spires said happily. "Usually I'm in a muck sweat, but yours seemed to want to cooperate."

Daphne stared, horrified, at the shrunken muscles of her legs. Would they ever again be the legs of a ballerina?

Maria said encouragingly, "With all them exercises wot the doctor's given us, you'll soon get rid of the crutches, luv."

At home, propped up on the Plonkit, Daphne picked up the sheet of diagrams and gritted her teeth. She'd learned to dance, hadn't she? So how difficult could this be? Slowly, she began to count out a rhythm. "One, two, three." Her legs were up, stretched out in front of her. "Four, five, six." She held them there. "Seven, eight, nine." They were down on the floor again. After doing it a few times, she was wringing wet with effort.

She heard a loud knock. The parlour door opened.

"DOLLY!" Daphne shouted.

"All right!" Dolly said, waving the *Hoxton Gazette* over her head. "You are a Friend after all!"

They hugged and then they both cried, and then Dolly sat down next to Daphne. "I've only come to stop Joe and Lofty nagging my head off," she said with a tremulous smile.

"So it wasn't the article?" Daphne asked.

"No. Ages before I saw it, I was trying to work out why I was still so angry with you, even though Joe kept going on about how you'd changed." Dolly mopped her eyes. "I was so muddled up. All the time I was still furious, I knew I was missing you, really."

"I don't blame you for being furious," Daphne said hurriedly. "I was such a horrible pig to you. Do you solemnly promise me, on your honour as a Friend, you've forgiven me?"

Dolly gave her a quick hug, then held out the *Gazette*. "I suppose you'd like to see the article about the wonder of you?" she said, smiling to show Daphne she was only teasing her.

Reg Paisley really had done Daphne proud. The front-page headline screamed: **SCOOP INTERVIEW WITH HOXTON'S FAMOUS BALLERINA!** The article itself covered the *Gazette's* two centre pages.

"Oh!" Daphne said quietly, folding up the paper. "They must have got that photograph of me in *The Scarlet Stockings* from the Ballet Splendide. I'll read it all later."

She stuffed the *Gazette* behind the velvet cushions of the Plonkit, took a deep breath, and said, "I'm starting straightaway. Strengthening and stamina exercises, just like taking a class, then organised times for rest and relaxation, until I'm strong enough to start dancing again. Here's the chart I'm trying to do."

Dolly's eyes widened. "You're really going to do this ten hours a day?"

"I won't be able to at first, but could you help me work it out so everything gets more intense as I get stronger?"

"Just my kind of problem," Dolly said enthusiastically.

Everyone marvelled at Daphne's relentless efforts. She got rid of her crutches and moved to a cane. At last, one morning, she walked and stood completely unsupported.

Just in time for when Magda comes to tea on Sunday, Daphne thought, triumphantly. *Might as well give the darling a chance for a bit of drama when she claps eyes on me!*

The parlour furniture had been polished until it shone. A table was so laden with Maria's home-made cakes, scones and sandwiches it looked as if it might collapse. Everyone except Daphne was feeling rather nervous but, just as she'd predicted, half an hour after Magda got to 52 Upper, Market Square, it was as if they'd known her all their lives.

"Mrs. G, this Bakewell tart is delicious," Magda said from her chair by the window. The afternoon sun made her diamond bracelets sparkle and put a halo around her shining blonde hair. "Could I be a shameful glutton and ask for another slice? I don't care if the buttons on my costume do pop off!"

The last of Maria's shyness melted away. "Glad you like it, luv," she said happily. "More tea for you, Mr. Crunge?"

"I wouldn't say no, thank you." Crunge undid the bottom button of his chauffeur's jacket. "And I'll take that recipe for Mrs. Crunge, if you'd be so kind."

Once the tea things were removed, Joe and Lofty cleared the room for Daphne's 'performance'. "First, I shall show you my amazing, death-defying walk!" she announced. Solemnly she circled the room, bowing to the applause. "Steady as a rock," she boasted. "And now for my big finale. Watch this!" Standing on one leg, holding onto the arm of the Plonkit, she stretched the other one straight out behind her in a reasonably steady arabesque. Then, amid breathless silence, she took away her supporting hand and balanced on her own.

This time, her audience leapt to its feet in a standing ovation! Unashamedly, Carlo wiped his eyes with a huge spotted handkerchief.

Magda flew across the room to hug Daphne. "Darling, I can see you're doing awfully well by yourself," she said, enthusiastically. "But if you're going to start dancing again, you must do it under the proper supervision. You're at the point now where you could really smash yourself up if you don't take the greatest of care. It's one thing to do limbering and warm-ups. You know better than anyone, it's quite another thing to work yourself back into dancing condition." She turned eagerly to Carlo and Maria, her eyes sparkling.

"I wonder would you let me kidnap Daphne back to Park Lane? Rudolf Gorky's prepared to work with her if she wants him to. I'd let her out of prison every weekend!"

"You're a genius, Magda! Why didn't I think of that?" Daphne said, alight with excitement. "But only on two conditions. Mr. Petrov has been awfully generous to me. Even though I couldn't dance, he's paid me for the whole of the rest of the season. So, I can afford my own lessons. The other thing is you must agree to let me start paying you back for everything else I owe you."

Joe beamed at Magda. "She won't sleep a wink tonight, you know!"

Drat Joe for saying she'd be awake all night with anticipation, Daphne stewed. Impatiently, she clicked on her bedside lamp.

Bother, she thought. *I'll have to read until I feel sleepy again.*

The *Hoxton Gazette* lay handy. Daphne reached for it. But when she came to the pages where the personal advertisements were, any possibility of closing her eyes at all that night vanished. The advertisement was only a small one, but every word held her rapt attention:

**COLLECTOR OF RARE BOOKS LOOKING FOR
COPY OF
'HOW TO TEACH YOURSELF BALLET'.
WRITE TO EMMA BROWN,WHITE PEAK FARM,
BAKEWELL, DERBYSHIRE.**

Chapter Twenty Eight

"I've never seen anywhere so green and so peaceful," Daphne sighed. She settled herself back in the Bakewell station taxi's cracked leather seat. Soft air drifted in through the open window. Scattered farms and little grey stone villages with beckoning names, like Stoney Middleton and Ashford-in-the-Water, drowsed in the sunshine as the rattling car passed them by. In the gently rolling hills, black-faced sheep nibbled the thick grass. Red grouse, their plumage glowing in the sunshine, searched diligently for worms in the rich soil of the fields.

For luck, Daphne had written *Knowing, you will challenge me* on a piece of paper. She had it, together with Emma Brown's advertisement, in the pocket of her dress. Summoning up all her courage, she vowed to bravely face whatever was waiting for her in this beautiful place.

"Soon have you at White Peak," the driver said, his countryman's face ruddy and cheerful. He pointed to a church with a pointed spire, clustered about with ancient, mellowed stone houses. "Ay, lass, that's Bakewell. You'll have 'eard of it, I expect."

"Well, I've eaten Bakewell tart!" Daphne said, craning her neck to stare, enchanted.

"You ask at the farm about Bakewell market," the driver advised. "We've 'ad it every Monday in the same place since the year 1300. The White Peak eggs and butter are very popular. Anyone'll tell you."

Studying Daphne's tense face in the rear-view mirror, he lapsed into tactful silence. He'd noticed she was very pale when she'd got into his taxi. Seeing her smart London clothes, his countryman's curiosity had been aroused. He'd wondered if the lass had been ill. Likely, she had come up to Derbyshire for a breath of good, clean air.

The taxi bumped along a narrow, rutted farm track, where deep hedgerows held out their masses of wild roses, sprays of feathery white Queen Anne's lace and bushes of ripening blackberries.

The postmark on the parcel said Rome, not an English farm hidden away up a hill, Daphne thought, confused, as a white five-barred gate and a faded signpost which read: WHITE PEAK FARM, came into view around a bend.

"I'll drop you, here, lass," the driver said, touching

his cap in thanks for the coins Daphne handed him. With a final interested stare, he drove off whistling, back down the lane.

A gentle late afternoon breeze and the soft baaing of a flock of nearby sheep accompanied Daphne as she opened the gate, walked slowly across the farmyard and, holding her breath, rapped with the brass knocker on the front door.

After a few long moments, it opened and a neatly dressed middle-aged woman appeared, wiping her hands on her apron. "Yes? Are you lost, miss?" she asked.

Daphne reached into her handbag and held out the advertisement. "I've come about this," she said, faintly.

The woman faltered, staring at Daphne, with a face that had gone the colour of old milk. "I'm Emma Brown," she said. "I think you'd best come in."

Suddenly, Daphne couldn't move. "Are you my mother?" The words blurted out in a panicked rush.

Emma stared, sadly, into Daphne's eyes. "No, luv, I'm not, but if you're who I think you are, I knew your mother well." Daphne's mind didn't seem to be working properly. She couldn't take any of this in. "Please, come in and sit down" Emma urged. "I know you haven't been well."

How does she know, Daphne wondered as, shaking, she followed the farmer's wife down a dark corridor and into a large, dim stone-floored kitchen, where a kettle purred to itself on an old-fashioned range.

"Who are you?" Daphne asked, urgently.

"I'm the person who left you at St. Jude's."

As the kitchen rocked around her, Daphne groped blindly for a chair. Emma handed her a glass of water, then sat down quietly facing her by a window, open onto the stables and barn.

The glass shook in Daphne's hand. "Please, would you tell me who my mother was," she whispered.

"Her name was Katerina Albemarle. I was her lady's maid." Emma had no need to say more. The whole world knew of the exquisite ballerina, dead so young of a heart disease.

Pride and joy rushed through Daphne in a dizzying wave. *My mother was Katerina Albemarle! She must have danced with me in her arms and longed for me to follow in her footsteps. So I was right all those times at St. Jude's when I was sure I wasn't just ordinary!*

But, almost immediately, with a sickening jolt, it hit her. St. Jude's! How and why had she come to be there? "Tell me everything. I've got to know absolutely everything," she said, leaning rigidly forward in her chair.

"I will," Emma said slowly. 'But I'm afraid it's going to hurt you."

Hurt me? How could anything hurt me more than growing up unwanted, Daphne thought, bewildered. "I don't care," she said passionately. "It's the most important thing in the world to me. Please, who was my father?"

Emma shook her head. "That I can't tell you. No one knew that. As soon as your mother realised she was pregnant, she made arrangements to leave the ballet in Rome for a season. We went to Frigiliana, a little village on top of a mountain in Spain. That's where you were born."

Reaching out a comforting hand, Emma said, "Be strong, luv. I'm right sorry to have to tell you this." She took a deep breath. "After you were born, she wouldn't even look at you. I begged her to hold you, to give you a name. But she ordered me to take you out of the room."

Once again, hopelessly, Daphne felt herself dropping into a lightless abyss. Her worst fears were true, after all. Her mother hadn't wanted her. No one had wanted her.

You idiot! You pathetic, daydreaming idiot! She wanted to yell the harsh, self-punishing words aloud. But she didn't. They stayed, ugly and echoing, inside her.

Gently, Emma continued, "Remember, love, she was a great star — people said the best ballerina in the world. I'd been with her for more than ten years. So, I knew how cold and secretive she could be. From the moment we left Rome I was frightened she'd decide to sacrifice the child — you — for her dancing. I couldn't imagine she'd let anything or anyone interfere with or interrupt that. And all those months in our little house in Spain I watched her getting angrier and quieter. It broke my heart but I was right." Emma paused, her face creased with worry and concern. "You're sure you want me to tell you everything?"

Daphne couldn't speak. She just nodded.

Emma's voice broke. "Your mother told me to take you away somewhere, anywhere, and swear on a Bible never to speak about you again to her or to anyone else."

Frightened by Daphne's deathly pallor, Emma said, "Shall I make you a nice cup of tea with some brandy in it?"

Daphne shook her head. An agonising pressure was building up behind her heart, a pain and anger so great she didn't know how she could possibly survive it. Shivering, she wrapped her arms around herself, struggling to bring some warmth back into her body.

"No, go on," she said in a scared whisper.

"I wrote to my Aunt Sarah in Hoxton for advice," Emma continued, her hand comfortingly on Daphne's arm. "She's the one in our family who always knows what to do. Of course I didn't tell her whose baby it was. She told me St. Jude's was a kind place. So, I gave you the name Daphne and I took you there. But I couldn't stay with your mother after that. I told her I wouldn't come back, but I'd always let her know where I was in case she changed her mind and wanted to find you."

"But she didn't," Daphne said dully. The unbearable pain she now felt made the physical injuries from her fall seem like shadows.

"No, luv, she didn't. She went back to Rome and her career. I didn't hear from her for years. Then the problems started with her heart. She went to doctors all over the world and they all told her the same thing. The damage had been caused by the strain of her dancing. She put everything she had into it. That's when she wrote and asked me to come to Rome. By then I was married to Colin and living here."

'By then.' 'Rome.' It was all beginning to make ugly sense. "And you went?"

"Yes, I went as soon as I could." Emma shook her

head sadly. "But when I got there she was already too weak to get out of bed. I could see something was tormenting her, so I asked her if she'd like to know where I'd taken you." Emma shivered. "I'll never forget the look on her face when she said, 'It's too late, Emma, much too late now.'"

Emma stopped and sighed. "There isn't much more, really, luv. She got much worse very suddenly. One of the last things I saw her doing was writing in that book. I watched her pushing herself to the limits of her strength to do it. Pitiful, it was. Then she asked me to bring her brown paper, scissors and some of the special silver string she always used.

"'Let me help you, Madam,' I begged. But she wouldn't. I saw her getting those red stockings of hers out from under her pillow. She always kept them close to her. When we travelled I was never allowed to touch them, she always packed them herself. I suppose she put them in the parcel for you, did she, luv? She sent me out of the room while she wrapped it, and we never found the stockings when we were packing up her things. I've always wondered what happened to them."

The aching knot in Daphne's throat was so bad she couldn't answer. She just nodded, and Emma went on.

"In a while your mother rang the little bell by her

bed. I came in and saw the package there. She hadn't the strength even to hand it to me. 'Emma, do one last thing for me. Send this to my daughter,' she said. Her voice was so weak I could hardly hear it."

A deep silence fell as Daphne and Emma sat, lost in their own thoughts. The only sound in the kitchen was the slow ticking of the grandfather clock in the corner. Then came a clatter of hooves outside the window. "That'll be Colin," Emma said, stirring. "He'll be a few minutes yet, settling the horse. Sit here, Daphne, nice and quiet. I've something to fetch for you."

She was back almost immediately. In her hand was a worn leather jewellery case. "It was hers," Emma said sadly, handing it to Daphne. "She never took it off, even when she was dancing."

The narrow woven gold bracelet gleamed in the soft light of the lamp by Daphne's chair. "She hoped you'd have it one day," Emma said softly. "The last thing she said to me was, 'It's impossible that my crimes towards my daughter could ever be forgiven. But if heaven, by some miracle, does relent it will send a sign. My daughter will come to you. When she does, give her this.'"

At Daphne's ragged gasp, Emma hurried on. "I've always hoped to give Fate a little push. So when Aunt

Sarah sent me the newspaper article about you it seemed like a signal, somehow. I had to do something. I thought if you were the same Daphne who'd got that parcel, you'd know all about the book. So me and Colin wrote the advertisement and sent it off. And you came, just as your mother hoped you would one day."

Slowly, Daphne picked up the bracelet. And threw it as hard as she could across the room. "DAMN my mother. And DAMN her bracelet. Am I supposed to feel sorry for her now? Because I don't. Why should I love her when she only loved herself? She was a heartless monster. I *hate* her, and I wish I'd never heard her name."

The kitchen door opened. Blindly Daphne rushed out, past the tall figure of Colin Brown, into the night.

A mist had risen, hovering over the fields. Daphne's stumbling feet crunched eerily over the farmyard's cobblestones. Angrily, she wiped her wet face with her sleeve as she fumbled open a gate and stood on the edge of a moonlit field.

Shivering, she fell to her knees, rocking backwards and forwards on the wet, spiky grass. So this was where all her hopes, her dreams had led her?

"Oh God, I hope I die here tonight," she cried up to the serene, unanswering moon.

PART FIVE

'At last, you must deserve me.'

Chapter Twenty Nine

When Daphne returned late the next evening from Derbyshire, Carlo and Maria were frightened by the dark circles under her eyes. "Straight to bed for you, luv, you can tell us all about it in the morning," Maria said.

Daphne gave them a look of such deep gratitude and love Carlo felt he might cry himself, and said gruffly, "That's right, I'll be in with your tea in the morning, as usual."

Just as the sun was rising next day, he came back to the kitchen, where Maria sat worriedly at the table. "It's orl right luv, don't worry, she slept in a farmhouse with some people she knows."

"She's never said nothing about anyone out in the country," Maria replied. Their troubled eyes exchanged a message. "I know." Maria sighed. "We've got to leave 'er alone. She'll tell us when she wants to."

In her darkened bedroom, Daphne lay hunched under the covers, her knees pulled in tightly to her chest. She wanted to be the smallest shape she could possibly make herself.

Perhaps she really was turning to ice. She'd welcome it, because then she could simply melt away, disappear to a place where betrayal and heartbreak couldn't touch her.

She didn't know how long she'd been in the field that night when she'd heard Emma's voice calling to her. "Daphne, come inside, luv, by the fire where it's warm."

Daphne hadn't been able to force a reply through her frozen lips, not even a harsh "Leave me alone". But Emma had found her anyway, had wrapped her in a shawl, and led her tenderly into the warmth, where the reassuring deep voice of Colin Brown had said, "Ee, lass, I'm that sorry you had to find out. We didn't know whether we should tell you, Emma and me, but we decided it wasn't our place to hide the truth from you, not once your mother was gone."

Daphne's rage had exploded out of her then. "Don't CALL her my mother!" she'd yelled. "She wasn't anybody's mother, she was a despicable human being. She left me year after year despising myself while she went on with her oh-so-wonderful life in complete happiness."

Emma had stretched out a comforting hand, but Daphne shoved it away. "Don't you UNDERSTAND?

Because of her I felt like a handkerchief someone had blown their nose into and then thrown away. She did her best to kill any feelings of love and trust I might ever be tempted to feel. She DESERVED to die in misery. I wish she'd suffered more — much, much more."

Emma and her husband hadn't tried to stop the bitter flow. They'd let Daphne cry and rage until she was so exhausted she could hardly stand up. Then Emma had put her to bed between lavender-scented linen sheets in a spare bedroom.

But Daphne hadn't slept more than half an hour at a time the whole night through. Her anger had become all tangled up with a bitter blanket of hurt. Each time she'd woken during that endless night she'd found the pillow sodden with her tears.

The morning came, as grey as the day before it had been sunlit. Although Emma had begged her to eat something before her journey back to Hoxton, Daphne hadn't been able to swallow so much as a drop of water. Her throat had closed up with stunned depression.

The journey to the station, sitting between Colin and Emma on the front seat of the farm's horse-drawn cart, had passed in almost complete silence.

The Browns had stood with Daphne on the deserted station platform. Needles of thin rain began to fall.

Finally, a bell clanged and the sound of a puffing engine had made itself heard around a bend in the track. As the locomotive came to a standstill, Emma had reached into her pocket and held out Katerina Albemarle's worn jewellery case.

Violently, Daphne shook her head.

"Take it, luv," Emma had urged. "It was left for you."

"Even if you never wear it, lass, it *is* yours," Colin had said quietly.

So, ungraciously, Daphne had taken the case from Emma's hand. "I'll always hate her, you know," she'd said. And those were the only words she'd spoken as Colin helped her into the carriage and put her little overnight bag up on the luggage rack.

After a moment or two Daphne had leaned out of the window to where the worried farmer and his wife stood on the platform.

"Thank you, both of you. I'll always remember how kind you've been to me," she'd said in a choked voice. And then the train had slowly moved away into the misty morning.

Almost miraculously, Daphne had the carriage all to herself the whole way to London. She sat in an agonising muddle. She hated her mother, she knew that for certain. So why did she still wish Katerina could appear, take her in her arms and say how proud she was that Daphne was her daughter?

Several times during the day Maria tiptoed to Daphne's door and put her hand on the knob. But the deep silence within sent her away, her face creased with worry, her offers of companionship, food and drink unspoken.

It wasn't until the evening that Daphne came out of her bedroom, her eyes puffy and swollen. She sat, huddled, on the Plonkit, hugging one of its soft, bulging cushions to her for comfort. Carlo, Maria and Joe sat quietly, listening.

"She never wanted me, even at the end. And when I think how every night I went to sleep longing for her and imagining all the reasons that were stopping her from coming to find me, I feel so stupid." Daphne's eyes filled again with angry tears. "And the worst thing of all," she said slowly, "is that in Paris I was just like her. Selfish and cold. Part of me hated myself, but the part that won was the part that admired how ambitious and clever I was being."

Brushing aside Maria's attempt at comforting words, Daphne said passionately, "It's taken me until now to realise that you're my real family. Real, not made up out of my head by childish wishing and dreaming."

"It's orl right, gel," Carlo said.

"No, it's NOT all right," Daphne burst out.

"Steady on!" Joe said, gently. "We know how you feel."

But, Daphne thought desperately, *they don't. There's so much I can't tell them. How can I thank them properly?*

The answer didn't come until weeks later. Towelling herself down after a class at the Gorky Studio of Dance, every muscle in her body screaming, Daphne noticed Gorky's appraising stare. "All right, Rudolf, tell me," she said affectionately. "I recognise that look on your face. You're hatching something!"

"Just trying to work out how many days are left," Gorky replied innocently. Each year, the well-known dancers in his classes raised money for dance scholarships by appearing in a gala at London's historic Theatre Royal.

Daphne felt sick. "*No*, Rudolf, please. I *can't*. It's much too soon."

The teacher put his hand on Daphne's shoulder. "One day you must dance in public again. And when you do, the fear will be the same, whether you dance for your friends in this room or for an audience in a crowded theatre."

Daphne was so scared her mind went blank. "I don't know, Rudolf, let me think," she whispered.

In the middle of the night, she woke in her room at Magda's, her head pounding. The idea that had come to her was completely extraordinary.

Sharing Magda's pot of breakfast tea, Daphne said tentatively, "I've been turning something over in my mind all night. I'd like to know what you think."

As she spoke, Magda became more and more appalled. "Daphne, DON'T!" she cried out in horror. "It will bring back the most terrible memories."

"But it would give Mum and Dad and the others so much pleasure. It would be a way of trying to make up for my horribleness in not even telling them I was dancing the role, or arranging for them to come to Paris for the opening night. It would be like a belated gift I could give them. But I'll have to tell Rudolf today, before I get a chance to change my mind." Daphne's voice shook.

Later that day, at the dance studio, Gorky raised his distinguished eyebrows. "Are you sure?" he asked.

"I'll *make* myself sure," Daphne answered.

"In that case, of course I'll help you. We must adapt it if you're dancing it as a solo. I don't have to tell you how hard you're going to have to work. We've got less than a month to do it."

* * *

Daphne had chosen to spend the night before the gala at home in Hoxton. In the morning, she sat in the kitchen, pushing a piece of toast around on her plate. It felt just like the day of her audition at the Splendide. She could almost smell the coffee and croissants.

The sound of rushing feet was followed by Joe banging open the kitchen door. "ARE YOU CRAZY? Wait till Ma and Pa see this!" he roared, flinging the *Gazette* down on the table.

BEAUTIFUL YOUNG DANCER'S BRAVE DECISION. WILL DANCE ROLE THAT ENDED HER CAREER!
By Reginald Paisley

Joe stared bleakly at the photo of Daphne in *The Scarlet Stockings*. "No wonder you've been so secretive about what you've been up to. You're doing this as a test, aren't you? You idiot, it's a test you don't have to take. You've already proved how brave you are." His face was as white as Magda's had been. "Don't be so damned stubborn. It's not too late to change your mind. Nobody would blame you for a moment."

He mustn't see how terrified I am, Daphne thought. She made her voice sound calm. "Joe, please. Nothing bad will happen. Encourage me for heaven's sake, instead of shouting at me."

He slumped down at the table. "I knew it wouldn't be any use talking to you. Honestly, Daphne, you can't expect us all to sit calmly in the audience and watch you, can you?"

"Joe, you don't understand. I'm doing this for you and Mum and Dad. I want to show you what you all mean to me."

"And I suppose falling into a big hole in the stage at the Theatre Royal is going to convince us of that, is it?" Carefree Joe was very, very scared.

The massive semi-circle of the Theatre Royal, with its four tiers of gilded balconies divided into curtained private boxes, its domed roof with the magnificent central chandelier and its portrait of the king over the golden arch of the stage, buzzed with excited speculation.

During the last months the newspapers had been full of Daphne's struggle to recover from her injuries. Once it was announced she'd be dancing for the first time since her appalling accident, the gala's remaining tickets had sold out in just hours.

Daphne stood, a fragile figure alone in the vast wings,

her head bent. Tentatively, she opened her hand. Katerina's bracelet lay there, as weightless as a teardrop. In weeks of passionate puzzling, during which time she'd reviewed her own past behaviour, her own choices, Daphne had slowly come to realise she felt pity in her heart for her mother. Just like herself, Katerina hadn't been strong enough, or loving enough, to resist the possibility of self-destruction that accompanied ownership of the scarlet stockings.

If I put the bracelet on tonight, it'll mean I've forgiven her in my deepest heart, Daphne told herself. She hesitated, still confused and uncertain. *I've got to be sure I really have. Forgiven her, with everything in me.*

As if on a stage, she saw a little girl, sobbing herself to sleep at St. Jude's. Then, suddenly, that spotlight went out and another went on as she bent, her heart pounding with strange anticipation, over a dusty cardboard box. Then, with a happy shiver, she was in a starlit market square, soaring up to the silver moon.

Suddenly elated, Daphne fastened the bracelet around her wrist with hands that no longer shook. As she gently touched the delicate circle of gold, the clouds of mystery vanished as if blown away by a refreshing wind.

At last, you must deserve me. Tonight, Daphne

278

understood the true meaning of the quest she had undertaken, the finding, the following, the choosing, the knowing and, now, the deserving.

With all her heart she gave thanks to Pierre Beauchamp for his riddle, the riddle that Katerina in her last moments had lovingly, remorsefully, bequeathed to her daughter as her real inheritance.

Daphne shivered. This was going to take all the courage she had.

Across the stage, in the far wings, Magda quietly motioned the Greens, Dolly and Lofty to follow her. They took their places, bunched together in a tight, nervous knot.

They've come backstage. Even more perfect! Daphne shook herself to settle her scarlet costume, so carefully recreated by Dolly for tonight's performance. With a swish, the curtains opened to complete and utter silence. Not a programme rustled, no one moved.

The conductor brought down his baton. Daphne flashed onstage, her opening series of spinning fouettés so incredibly fast and perfect the audience gasped. The applause started. As she danced, a shining miracle of beauty in motion, it became a great roar.

The Scarlet Stockings solo drew to its close as its heroine ran from the stage in madness and despair. To the continuous screaming of violins, the braying of the brass and the sombre roll of drums the curtains drew shut, then opened again on the lurid sky, the slashing streaks of lightning, the high crag and the yawning abyss. Daphne's scarlet figure spun back into view high above the stage.

In the stalls the dance critics sent their pencils flying across their notebooks. Something entirely magical was happening in front of their eyes tonight.

As Daphne gathered herself for her final leap, the audience seemed to stop breathing and a noise that sounded like a long "Aaaaaaah" filled the vast space.

Daphne's feet left the ground. Up and up and up she soared.

"Catch me!" she called out softly into the wings.

And, instead of falling in despair into the terrifying, lonely chasm, she flew joyfully across it and into the arms of the people she loved and trusted most in the world.